Raindrops on Radishes

VALERIE COMER

GreenWords Media

ACKNOWLEDGMENTS

Thank you for being a faithful reader of the Urban Farm Fresh Romance series!

Kudos to Jessica and Mike Kovac of Blessings Under the Bridge, a real ministry to the real homeless in the real city of Spokane, Washington. Thank you for your insight and permission to use your ministry fictiously in this novel. I pray God's blessing on you. Readers, check them out here: http://www.butb.org/.

Much appreciation to Wally from Market Gardening (dot com) for answering questions on the legalities of gardening in other people's backyards.

Trim Healthy Mama is also real. It's a faith-based way-of-eating that has helped hundreds of thousands of women and their families lose weight and find freedom. While Sadie's experience is fictional, it is similar to many I've read by my fellow travelers in my own journey to renewed health. Check them out at http://trimhealthymama.com.

Thanks to my beta readers, who helped me walk the fine line in two sensitive subjects, obesity and adoption. I appreciate you, Elizabeth Maddrey, Paula, Amy, Esther, and Joy. I hope I have done justice to your comments and input. They made the story so much stronger.

A big thank you to my fabulous editor, Nicole, who sees beyond words, punctuation, and sentence structure to the heart of the story.

I'm also grateful for the Christian Indie Authors Facebook group and my sister bloggers at Inspy Romance. These folks make a difference in my life every single day. I'm thrilled to walk beside them as we tell stories for Jesus!

Thank you to my Facebook friends, followers, street team, and reader group members for prayers, encouragement, and great fellowship.

Thanks to my husband, Jim, for research trips to Spokane and talking through scenarios as needed — to say nothing of everyday love and support — and to my kids and grandgirls for cheering me on and embracing the idiosyncrasies of having an author for a mom and grandmother.

All my love and gratitude goes to Jesus, the One who invited me to experience His unending and passionate love and walks beside me every day. My prayer is that you see His love anew through the pages of this story.

Valerie Comer Bibliography

Urban Farm Fresh Romance

0. Promise of Peppermint (ebook only)
1. Secrets of Sunbeams
2. Butterflies on Breezes
3. Memories of Mist
4. Wishes on Wildflowers
5. Flavors of Forever
6. Raindrops on Radishes
7. Dancing at Daybreak

Saddle Springs Romance

1. The Cowboy's Christmas Reunion
2. The Cowboy's Mixed-Up Matchmaker
3. The Cowboy's Romantic Dreamer
4. The Cowboy's Convenient Marriage

Christmas in Montana Romance

1. More Than a Tiara
2. Other Than a Halo
3. Better Than a Crown

Garden Grown Romance
(Arcadia Valley Romance)

1. Sown in Love (ebook only)
2. Sprouts of Love
3. Rooted in Love
4. Harvest of Love

Farm Fresh Romance

1. Raspberries and Vinegar
2. Wild Mint Tea
3. Sweetened with Honey
4. Dandelions for Dinner
5. Plum Upside Down
6. Berry on Top

Riverbend Romance Novellas

1. Secretly Yours
2. Pinky Promise
3. Sweet Serenade
4. Team Bride
5. Merry Kisses

valeriecomer.com/books

CHAPTER 1

*T*here's a man in the backyard." Sadie Guthrie peered out the small window in the back stairwell, clutching her cell phone to her ear. "Why would someone come into my yard uninvited?"

"What's he doing?" Denae asked. "I mean, if he's walking toward the door..."

"He's not." Sadie shifted a little. Maybe her vision was obscured by the stained-glass bluebirds gliding in a circle of slightly wavy clear glass. "He's... digging?"

"You're kidding, right?"

Could the distortions mess up her eyes that much? Not possible, but having another peek from the kitchen window before she hung up on her best friend and called the police seemed like a good idea. "I'm going downstairs to get a better look."

"I'll stay on the line. Because what if he's hiding a body there? You might be his next victim."

"Or you might read too many mystery and suspense novels." Sadie entered the kitchen and angled a look out the window above the sink, taking care to stay in the shadows in case the man looked up.

"You okay? Is he still there?" Denae's voice prompted.

"I'm okay. And he's definitely not digging a hole deep enough for a body. It looks more like he's... gardening."

"Did you say *gardening*?"

"Yeah. But who does that in someone else's yard?" There'd been signs, though, when she bought the place. Denae and her cousin had hurried Sadie through the house when they came to clean out their grandmother's lifetime of collections.

Sadie had signed papers on the spot. This was exactly the sort of heritage home she'd been looking for all over Spokane, Washington. That she'd be only ten minutes from her office downtown while living in a quiet neighborhood backing a steep hillside had sealed the deal. She didn't even mind the throwback kitchen, which didn't match the era of the house one iota. It wasn't like she cooked, so how bad could it be?

Her brain clicked that Denae rapid-fired questions at her. "How old is he? How is he dressed? Is he looking around to see if he's being watched?"

"Um, he looks maybe thirtyish? Dark curly hair brushing the collar of an old denim shirt. Scruffy jeans."

"I guess mass murderers can start at any age."

"Denae. Stop it. You're scaring me."

"I'm praying protection around you. Has Grandma's landline been disconnected yet? Because I'll stay right here while you call 9-1-1."

"They removed the wires this morning."

"Maybe you can go out the front door and make the call

from a safe place, like next door. Only what if they're in on it, too?"

"In on what?"

The man stood and stretched from side to side then leaned on the handle of a long spade and glanced around. He did look rather suspicious. Could Denae's over-active imagination be right, just this once?

"It could be a crime ring. If not murder, maybe drugs. Or maybe he's going to bury the cash or jewels from a heist and frame you for it!"

"Denae. Don't even—"

"You can't be too careful."

Decades ago this neighborhood under the bridge had been a magnet for addicts and the destitute. Sadie might not have spent more than an hour in the house before signing papers, but she'd researched Bridgeview along with every other area of Spokane in her year-long quest. She'd missed an opportunity for a riverside home near here just last summer by pondering too long, and she hadn't been about to make that mistake again. Not when the price was so reasonable, and the old woman's family hadn't even listed it with a real estate agency yet.

Win, win.

Maybe.

The man turned as he looked around, a crease furrowing his brow. Even with the frown, he was awfully cute. His denim-clad shoulders were broad, his sleeves rolled up to reveal tanned muscles in his forearms. Who in the Inland Northwest had a tan by the end of March? The snow had only finished melting away a few weeks ago.

She knew the moment he realized something was off.

His gaze sharpened on the collapsed cardboard boxes beside the back door. He scanned the back of the house again, and Sadie stepped even further into the shadows lest he could see six feet deep into the unlit kitchen.

Denae's jabbering faded into meaningless, rolling sounds.

He strode toward the porch.

Sadie gripped the phone with a sweaty hand. What a stupid design for a house! There was no escape from the kitchen without being in full view of that back door. She heard his footsteps cross the deck. Heard the sharp knock.

There was no place to hide. She let out a shaky breath. "Denae?"

"Are you okay?"

"I-I'm not sure. He's coming to the door. I'm going to set the phone down a few feet away and go answer it, okay? Don't leave me."

"I've got your back. If he messes with you, he'll pay. I promise I won't let your death go unavenged. Just a sec. I'll start recording."

Another knock sounded, louder this time.

"Stay quiet so he won't know you're listening."

"Mum's the word."

The door creaked open. "Mrs. Essery? Are you home?"

That had been the former owner's name. Was this guy on walk-in-without-invitation terms with the old woman?

Sadie tapped the icon for speaker and set the phone down on the counter, but her shaking hands missed. The device clattered to the scuffed wooden floor.

The intruder's gaze swung to meet hers.

THE WOMAN STARING BACK at Peter Santoro was definitely not Beulah Essery. She was fifty years younger, considerably rounder, and a whole lot prettier, for starters.

"Sadie? What happened? Are you there? Or I'm calling the police." A panicked voice squawked from the phone.

The woman — Sadie? — grabbed the phone. "Sorry. It fell on the floor. Hang on a minute." She straightened, her gaze never leaving his as she set the device on the counter. "Who are you and what are you doing in my backyard?"

Peter blinked. "*Your* backyard?"

Her blue eyes shot fire at him. "Yes. I bought this house. You're trespassing."

"Uh uh. Beulah and I have an agreement. She'd let me know when she was ready to sell, and I'd buy it."

She shook her head. "Beulah Essery passed away two weeks ago."

No way. This woman had to be lying. Or Peter was having a nightmare. That was it. He'd wake up in a few minutes and share the story with Alex over morning coffee. They'd both have a good laugh before Peter came next door to sow the second planting of radishes. Right?

The woman didn't seem like a dream. She looked very real with her shoulder-length blond curls, white pleated top, and navy jacket and slacks. Heels. If Peter were imagining a woman, she'd be in jeans and a cute T-shirt. He'd never come up with this business look in the middle of the night.

She must be real, then. Which meant her story might be, too.

He needed to think, because the conversation had gone

way off script. He stuck out his hand. "I'm Peter Santoro, and I live next door, renting a room from my cousin Alex. I've known Beulah most of my life. Last I heard from her, she was enjoying an extended visit with her family in Cannon Beach."

"I'm Sadie Guthrie. Mrs. Essery's granddaughter Denae is one of my closest friends."

"Hi there." The female voice crackled from the phone at Sadie's elbow.

He gave the device a sidelong look. "Uh... hi." Weird.

"Denae and I were chatting when I saw you in the yard. She's still on the line." Sadie raised her eyebrows at him.

Like he was supposed to read some significance in that?

"Yeah, I'm a witness, so don't try any funny stuff."

Peter blinked. "Funny stuff?" What on earth? They thought he was... what? He couldn't help the chuckle that erupted.

"Not so fast, buster," the disembodied voice warned.

He held up both hands as he corralled his mirth. "No villainous purposes. I was simply tending my garden when I noticed the packing boxes on the porch and came to check on Beulah."

A perplexed frown graced Sadie's face. "Tending your garden? This is my house. My yard."

Worry gnawed at Peter's gut. "I have an arrangement with Beulah. I care for her yard, growing berries and vegetables, and she gets all the fresh produce she wants." One thing at a time. He'd address the purchase pact after his livelihood was secured.

Sadie took a step closer, a faint scent of vanilla tickling his nostrils. "You may have had an agreement with her, but she's dead and her legal heirs sold the property to me. You and I—" she motioned between them "—don't have an agreement. While I'm sure the family appreciates you looking out for their grandmother, the situation has changed. Your... services... are no longer needed or wanted."

"*You're* the one who doesn't understand. Beulah signed..."

She rolled her eyes. "I'm not sure if you're always this dense or if today is a special occasion." She pointed at official-looking paperwork on the counter behind her. "I. Own. This. Property. The prior owner's agreements are no longer valid. I'll thank you to remove your, your shovel and your presence from my yard, or I'll call the police."

"Go, Sadie!" called the voice from the phone.

Who was that person again? Peter snatched up the cell. "You're Mrs. Essery's granddaughter? Didn't she explain her wishes to her family? She promised to sell me the property." He'd let the details of the elderly woman's demise sink in later. For now, he had a garden to protect and real estate to gain possession of. Could someone be forced to unbuy a house?

"Yes, I'm Denae Archibald. Beulah's daughter Myrna is my mom."

"And didn't she tell all of you what she wanted?" She had to have. Peter was grasping at straws. He knew it, but what choice did he have? He couldn't just walk away from two seasons of hard work. From all his dreams for Bridgeview Backyards, the business he co-owned with his cousin Jasmine. They needed everything to go right this season after dipping into their savings to buy out Jasmine's brother. Cash flow was a mere trickle until sales rose. And sales couldn't rise without produce for sale.

"She did mention that the nice boy next door had approached her about buying her out."

Peter's teeth ground in frustration. "Then why...?"

"My uncle Ted is the executor, and he was determined to liquefy all assets as quickly as possible. Sadie made an offer for the house and its contents, and Uncle Ted accepted it on behalf of the estate. Done deal."

"But you can't." There was simply no way on God's green earth that this could be happening.

"Sorry." Denae's voice held no remorse.

He'd counted on this house next door so much they'd planted perennials here. Berries. Asparagus. Varieties that required several years to establish and could not easily be moved. They'd lose the income while transplanting and waiting for new growth.

Peter didn't bother pressing the button to end the call as he plunked the phone back on the counter. Let Denae keep listening. She wanted to be a witness? Fine, then. Let her.

"This isn't over." He stared Sadie straight in the face, steeling himself against her vanilla fragrance and focusing instead on her blue eyes, as unyielding as his own. "I have a signed agreement, and I'll be taking it to my attorney."

At least, if he had one. Alex's kid brother was in his third year of law school. That counted, right? It had to be enough for some advice.

"I won't be hiring an attorney," Sadie informed him. "I won't need one."

From the cell phone, Denae snickered.

The nerve. Peter raised his eyebrows. "I think you will." No way was he letting on his bravado was mostly bluff. Surely the agreement would hold up. Their marketing consultant — the guy who'd wound up marrying Peter's business partner — had harped on formal, signed contracts with the various landowners Bridgeview Backyards dealt with, so they'd typed something up and taken copies around. None had been notarized. Still, the contracts proved intent. That might be enough. It had to be.

A faint smile crossed Sadie's features.

Too bad it wasn't more reassuring.

"You misunderstand. I won't need representation, because I am a lawyer myself."

Peter felt the nails secure his coffin with every word.

CHAPTER 2

*S*adie forced the smirk off her face as panic bubbled up in the cute guy's eyes. He opened his mouth and closed it a few times, like a fish in a glass bowl. There was an idea. Fish were relaxing, low-stress pets, right? She should get a few. She'd sit with the lights out, mesmerized by the slow swishes in a gently lit aquarium. That would take her anxiety down a notch or two right there.

It needed taking down. All this stress wasn't good for her. Stress like some random guy digging up her backyard. "Come to Bridgeview," they said. "It's a quiet, safe neighborhood where neighbors look out for one another." No one had mentioned they looked out for one another to the point of digging up each other's yards uninvited.

Here came the stress headache again. She needed to get rid of this man — permanently — take some painkillers, and get back to moving in. Any relaxing on her agenda required her house to be a peaceful oasis first.

She wasn't an attorney for nothing. She could think and stare down this guy at the same time. One eyebrow carefully quirked — it had taken an entire reading week in front of the mirror to perfect that technique — and confidence oozing from every pore.

Imagine he's a deadbeat dad. An abusive foster parent. A wealthy citizen demanding she hush a high-profile case.

Her chin came up.

But she didn't have Denae's imagination. She couldn't quite picture this man in any of those capacities. Short brown hair, but long enough for a woman to run her fingers through. *Stop it, Sadie!* A neatly trimmed beard. And intense blue eyes, the color of her Siamese cat's.

Peter visibly pulled himself together. "I'm sorry to hear of Beulah's passing. I didn't know her well, but she seemed a fine woman and good neighbor."

Sadie would be a good neighbor, too, if guys like him weren't digging up her backyard. Talk about making a poor first impression. "I only met her a few times, when she'd visit Denae's family."

Denae. She was still listening. "Speaking of whom..."

"If you're absolutely certain you're going to be all right, I've got a novel calling my name."

Sadie didn't let her gaze slip from Peter's face. "Everything is fine. I can handle this."

"Call me later." Then silence from the cell phone on the counter.

Peter shifted from one foot to the other. "I'm sure we can work something out."

She smiled. "There's nothing to work out, actually. This is my home. I have a clear title." Well, she and Wells Fargo Bank, but whatever. "You say you provided Beulah all the vegetables she wanted, but as I don't really cook, that's not an incentive for me. And since it *is* my property, I expect you to clear your plants and paraphernalia off it as soon as possible. Say, by the end of the weekend?"

"You don't cook?"

Out of all she'd said, *that* was what stood out to him? "It seems I never acquired the knack, and now? Frankly, I'm too busy."

"Lawyering."

"Exactly."

"If you're so all-fired busy, wouldn't it be a blessing to have your yardwork covered? Think of not having to mow, or weed, or trim bushes. I can take care of everything back there."

Persistent. The guy should've gone to law school himself. She tapped her jaw, pretending to think over his offer. "You're right that I'm not really into mowing."

His face brightened.

She held up a hand. "I've got a landscaper coming in to evaluate the space and give me a quote. I'm thinking a large patio with a shade structure. Maybe a fountain, since the bubbling sound is such a good destressor. Flower gardens chosen for the scent of their blossoms. Natural aromatherapy, also a good relaxant." She could imagine reading her Bible and praying in such a peaceful oasis. "The landscaper will handle the upkeep."

Peter's mouth opened and closed. "But—"

"Vegetables are great in their place." She lowered her voice, keeping it gentle. "This is not their place." Neither was their place on her plate, for the most part. Give her a cinnamon roll from that bistro down by the river any day of the week over a stick of celery.

"This isn't a good time of year to move plants."

Nice try, buster. "I'm sorry." But not sorry enough to change her mind.

"The asparagus will be ready to pick in a couple of weeks then will keep producing for over a month. It's a perennial that takes two to three years to become established."

The band around her head tightened. Her patience was *this* thin. "You'll need to give your sob story to someone else, Mr. Santoro. You mentioned your lawyer. Have her get in touch."

"Her?"

"Your lawyer."

"Oh. Him."

Sadie lifted a shoulder. Of course. It was still a male-dominated field, but she couldn't help goading the man. "Since we have nothing further to say to each other, I suggest you leave the property now, unless you're ready to begin removing your plants this morning."

He straightened, and the blue eyes went straight to icy chill. "I'm not rolling over and giving up quite that easily. Don't get your hopes up."

"Your call. I'm a very busy woman, Mr. Santoro. I've taken this week away from the office to get settled in. Feel free to begin removal any time." She leaned in a little. He took a step back. A twinge of guilt assaulted her, but she pressed on. "However, I want you to know that if I see any sign at all that you are proceeding with any task other than removal, I will press charges immediately, and your grace period will be over. Am I clear?"

"Very clear, ma'am." He pivoted on one heel and strode out the door, clicking it firmly shut behind him.

Sadie watched through the window as he shouldered his spade and exited the gate on the east side of the yard, which led to the space next door. A backyard where there wasn't a stitch of grass to be seen, only an array of raised garden beds marching across it with neat rows of early spring growth. A small patio housing a grill on a stand peeked out from behind a garden shed. There wasn't a tree on the place.

What a way to live, devoting one's life to growing vegetables to the exclusion of everything else. He said he lived with his cousin? How many veggies could a couple of guys eat, anyway?

Her gut sank. Just her luck to move in next door to a cute guy or two and discover they were vegetarians. Maybe even vegans. Sure, she ordered a salad sometimes for lunch, when guilt overcame her, but that was about it. She'd ignore the fact that the breaded chicken, croutons, and a double glug of creamy dressing probably negated any health benefits.

She turned from the window. Hot men, not that she was looking, shouldn't be vegetarians. End of story.

⁓

"TELL ME WHAT TO DO." Even the aroma of grilled steak didn't have the power to lure Peter to the table. "Somebody solve this already. Evan?"

Jasmine, his cousin and business partner, pointed her fork at Peter. "Sit. Eat."

"I can't. It all looks like sawdust. This is crazy." He drove his hands through his hair and pivoted at the window. "All our work gone down the drain. Unless we have a hope of overturning her purchase of the house."

At Peter's panicked phone call, Evan, Jasmine, and Nathan had joined him and Alex for dinner. His cousin could be counted on to bring an in-season salad. In this case it included radishes from the backyard and imported cucumbers. There was a limit to how much growing magic a team could pull off in the Inland Northwest in April.

Evan heaped more potato salad on his plate and grabbed another sourdough roll Peter had picked up at the bistro. A student never passed up free food. Even, apparently, a law student who lived in his parents' basement with room and board tossed in. "Show me your agreement with Mrs. Essery?"

Nathan made a strangled sound as Peter strode to the filing cabinet just off the eat-in kitchen. Yeah, yeah, he knew they hadn't dotted every *i* and crossed every *t*. Third drawer. Halfway back. He pulled out a thin folder and handed it to Evan, who pushed his plate aside slightly to peruse the contents.

Evan's eyebrows quivered.

Sort of like Peter's gut.

"This is all you guys have?" Evan looked between him and Jasmine.

Nathan leaned back in his chair and crossed his arms.

Peter remembered all the times Nathan had pushed the issue. "That's it."

"We always meant to get back to it and create more formal agreements." Jasmine parked her elbows on the table. "Then when Basil got his DUI and was sent to jail, all our plans were dumped upside down."

"Yeah." Peter scratched his head, carefully not looking at Nathan. "It doubled our workload, and we had to buy him out, so we didn't really have the funds to get all these done up properly and notarized. Alex knows."

Of Jasmine's four brothers, Alex was the up-and-coming hotshot accountant at a large firm downtown and the financial advisor of their fledgling business, Bridgeview Backyards.

"And it didn't seem necessary." Jasmine shot him a glance. "I mean, we know all our landowners. Who was going to kick us off?"

Peter nodded. "Beulah was only, what, seventy-two or something? She was the picture of health when she drove to the coast last month to visit her kids. We sure weren't expecting her to die."

Evan snapped the folder shut. "You can make all the excuses you want, but that doesn't magically replace these scraps of paper with legal contracts. If that lawyer woman bought Mrs. Essery's house, she owns the land and has a right to do whatever she wants with it." He gave a lopsided grin as he smacked the file into Peter's hand like a gavel. "Case closed." He pulled his plate closer and forked a large bite of salad into his mouth.

Peter looked at the beige folder in his hands then at Jasmine. "What do we do now?"

She stared back at him unmoving. Unspeaking.

Evan swallowed. "You either make a deal with the new owner, or you dig up your plants from her yard like she asked you to."

The woman hadn't *asked*. It had been more like a court order. "I need another option." Peter knew he was scrambling.

"There is no door number three." Evan glanced at Alex. "Good steak, by the way. You the chef?"

Alex nodded, but he wore a worried frown. "I guess the first order of business should be to make sure it can't happen again. Get the rest of those agreements legalized."

"There's only so much you can do." Evan eyed the serving bowls. "The only thing that might have saved you here is acquiring the right of first refusal to buy any property in question before it is offered to the public. Otherwise, no agreement you make will hold up with a new landowner. At least not beyond harvesting the current year's crops. Can someone pass the potato salad, please?"

"We don't want to buy all the places we're gardening on," Jasmine protested. "We can't afford to, anyway. We were hoping to expand to ten or more yards."

"Then the best thing is to make sure that you only grow annuals on someone else's land." Evan eyed the steak on Jasmine's plate. "You going to finish that, sis?"

She pushed it at him. "Go ahead."

He poked at it. "Might need to throw this back on the grill for a few minutes. I think I hear it saying 'moo'."

Alex glared at his kid brother. "Cook it yourself then."

"Don't mind if I do." Evan pushed back his chair and headed out the back door.

Nice Evan had an appetite. Peter sure didn't. How could this have happened? Beulah hadn't been that old, though older than Peter's uncle who'd been killed in an accident last fall. Life came with no guarantees. The seasons rolled on, regardless.

Summer and winter, and springtime and harvest. Sun, moon, and stars in their courses above join with all nature in manifold witness to Thy great faithfulness, mercy and love. All I have needed, Thy hand has provided...

The words from the old hymn tumbled through Peter's mind. God remained in control, even when his business took another blow. Yes, he'd known better than to plant berry bushes and asparagus on someone else's land, even though Beulah had promised him first dibs on the purchase when she was ready to sell in five or ten years. But it had been so convenient, right next door to Alex's, and he was going to own it, anyway. Peter had been carried away with his idyllic vision.

It had crashed and burned.

You either make a deal with the new owner, or you dig up your plants from her yard like she asked you to.

She refused to make a deal. He refused to dig up the asparagus. Why wasn't there a third choice? There had to be one.

Peter stuck the file back in the cabinet and crossed to the front window with its view of rooftops descending to the Spokane River a few blocks away. The third alternative might be trying to romance the woman.

He managed to keep from snorting out loud.

There wasn't anything enticing about Ms. Guthrie. Nothing welcoming. If he arrived on her doorstep asking for a date, she'd probably call the cops. She'd never believe he didn't have ulterior motives.

Because he did. He wanted access to that backyard. He wanted that house.

Maybe he should swallow his pride and talk to his dad about co-signing a loan. Surely he could make an offer for the property she'd accept. She'd move out, he'd move in, and all would be well. He'd been saving money from his job with Washington Department of Fish and Wildlife, the job he'd hoped to give up in a couple of months to go full-time with his and Jasmine's start-up. He'd had to dip into those savings to buy out Basil. He really wasn't in a good position to purchase a house right now, but maybe with his parents' help?

That went against the grain. If Alex could buy his own place at only twenty-four, Peter felt like a loser asking his folks for assistance at twenty-eight. He wasn't a kid. He should be able to figure things out on his own.

Losing the house next door went even deeper against the grain, though.

Enticing Sadie Guthrie to sell it to him was door number three. Trying to date her definitely was a bad idea, doomed to failure.

He didn't mind women with a little extra padding, but a hard-nosed attorney who hated vegetables was not his idea of a fun date. To say nothing of one date not being enough. He'd have to marry her to get the house.

So not happening. It was like door number eighty-nine. If only there were that many options.

Next stop, talking to his parents... which he should have done long ago rather than leaving the situation in limbo.

CHAPTER 3

"Your mom would have been so proud of you, honey."

Sadie stiffened as she preceded Stan down the stairs after giving him a tour of her new home. "You mean the woman who wasn't my mother?"

He sighed. "She was your mother in every way that counted. We adopted you. Raised you as our own. Gave you the best of everything."

"Except the truth."

"Sadie..."

"Don't. I'm sure you meant well. Let's just call her Lynda, okay? I can accept having had Lynda in my life, but she wasn't Mom." Never mind that Sadie had called her that for sixteen years. "I'm sure you rescued me from a life on the streets with a drug-and-sex addicted teen mom, but didn't anyone counsel you back then that not even telling a child she was adopted was a bad idea?"

"We had our reasons."

"I'm sure you did. I hear them in my office and in the

courtroom all the time." The day Lynda died had changed Sadie's life forever. She'd already been considering law school, but the upheaval in her family dynamics had sent her into family law. Kids needed protecting from the adults in their lives. Needed an advocate. That someone was Sadie Guthrie... or whatever her original name really was.

"Can we agree to set this old argument aside permanently?" Stan sounded tired. "It's not like I can go back and do anything differently. I'm sorry you felt blindsided with the information."

Sadie rubbed her temples and led the way back through the formal dining room with its walnut table, straight-backed chairs, and china cabinet. The family had removed the personal contents, but no one had wanted the furniture. It wasn't Sadie's favorite, either, but at least the house wasn't bare. She could replace the pieces room by room as she honed her vision for the interior spaces.

Her conscience poked her. She knew better than to goad Stan. He might not have been the kind of father who nurtured her by coming to dance recitals or flying kites with her, but he'd provided for her. Lynda had tried. It wasn't like Sadie had been beaten or deprived. Still, Lynda's dying words had confirmed everything she'd always felt. She hadn't belonged. Even with all the connections she'd forged in the decade since, she'd only run into brick walls trying to unearth her own origins.

Whatever Stan knew about her roots, he wasn't saying. Said it wasn't his place. Oh, really? Then whose place was it? No one else in her life held any of the pieces. Just him.

"I'm sorry." Sometimes a person had to preserve the

peace. "Can I fix you a coffee? I picked up some treats from the bakery down the hill."

He glanced at her body, his jaw tightening. "A coffee would be nice, thanks."

Why didn't he just come out and tell her she was fat? That she didn't measure up in any way? Just because he was six-foot-two and skinny as a pole.

"Sure. Have a look at the tower by the coffee maker and pick a flavor."

"Just regular is fine, if you have it. Black."

Now he was going to judge her for indulging in a caramel espresso. Whatever. She slipped a medium roast pod into the machine, turned it on, and turned to face Stan. "How long are you in town?"

He held her gaze for long enough it made her nervous. "I thought I'd relocate here. I'm retired. I can live wherever I want."

Sadie would have wobbled if she weren't leaning on the counter. "You're moving? Why?"

"Because you're my only child. My only family. Now that you've bought a house, it looks like you're staying here."

He'd asked her to apply at law firms along the coast last year, closer to Cannon Beach. Closer to him. She didn't want to live close to him. Eastern Washington wasn't even far enough away from western Oregon. She bit her lip. "I see."

"Look, I know you don't want me, but I want to do right by you. I want to be around when you have a family. I'm not asking to hang out every night or be part of everything. I just want to know I'm nearby if you need me."

Sadie sucked in her lower lip. Shouldn't his words make

her feel loved? Cared for? But they didn't. She didn't want him around. Did that mean she wanted to be alone forever? But she had Jesus... and Anastasia. How many cats did it take to become a crazy cat lady? Pretty sure more than one, though a Siamese probably counted double for attitude.

Stan sighed. "I promise I won't buy the house next door."

She forced a chuckle. "Go for it. I wouldn't mind different neighbors."

"Oh? Loud partiers or what?"

At least he'd understood it wasn't that she actually wanted him next door. "No, for a few guys, they're pretty quiet, so far." She just kept waiting for the other shoe to drop. She hadn't seen Peter since Saturday morning, and in those four days, nothing had changed in her backyard. Not that she knew what was Mrs. Essery's work and what was Peter's.

Stan nodded. "I'll give a real estate agent a call tomorrow and see what's available. Nothing's decided yet."

"I see." Maybe it wouldn't be so bad. He did try. He had no idea, really, of how to treat her, just like she had no idea how to treat him. Maybe now that she was an adult with her own home and a solid career, they could create some kind of relationship. It wouldn't be anything like her friends and their dads, but Stan was right. Not only was she all he had, she had no one else, either. No one she'd been able to find in all her searching.

The coffee pot gurgled to a halt, and she handed him his cup before restarting it with a flavored pod. She hesitated beside the box of cinnamon rolls. Stan wouldn't stay long.

She'd have one of those as a reward when he returned to the hotel.

The front doorbell rang.

Sadie frowned as she navigated through the formal rooms, turned the lock, and pulled the door open.

A middle-aged man smiled and extended his hand. "Hi, Ms. Guthrie? I'm Garry Bertoli with Century 21, and I'm wondering if you might be interested in selling your home."

"Selling my...?" Sadie flinched and took a step back. "Why would you think that? I haven't even been moved in for a full week."

The man's white-strip smile did not waver. "I have a client looking for a heritage home just like this one. He's willing to pay well. You could flip it for a profit, if you're interested."

"Thanks, but no thanks. I was looking for a heritage home just like this one myself, and I found it. I'm not going anywhere for a good many years to come."

Garry Bertoli held a business card toward her. "Give me a call if you change your mind."

Sadie crossed her arms over her chest. "I said I'm not interested. Please get off my property."

"Have a good day, ma'am." He tipped an imaginary hat then strode back to his black car sitting by the curb.

Why would anyone think she'd want to sell when she'd only just moved in? Her eyes narrowed as she took in the house next door. Peter's trump card? If so, she'd won the battle.

PETER TAPPED the icon to end the call and turned to Jasmine and Nathan. He'd gone over to their house after work rather than home, so his next-door neighbor couldn't pin it on him. "That was Garry. No dice."

"It was a long shot." Jasmine sighed.

"It might be time to admit defeat." Nathan straddled a kitchen chair and rolled up his shirt sleeves.

Jasmine shook her head. "Peter's right. We can't give up."

Nathan raised his eyebrows. "I can't condone you sneaking into someone else's yard and gardening at night, love. It's not our property."

"There's one more thing to try," Peter said slowly. He was going to hate himself for even going here.

Jasmine planted both hands on her hips. "Oh?"

He rubbed his short beard. "I could, uh, ask her out."

A hoot of laughter exploded from Nathan. "You what?"

"I'm with my husband here." Jasmine rested her hands on Nathan's shoulders and began to massage them. "Is she pretty? Are you actually attracted to her?"

"Well, she's about our age, give or take a couple of years, and apparently single. It seems it couldn't hurt to give it a try."

"You would date a woman to get her house?" Nathan chuckled. "This is not anything I ever expected out of a guy like you."

"A guy like me? What is that supposed to mean? I'm up against the wall here. We need that yard."

Jasmine dug her strong fingers so deep into Nathan's muscles the guy winced. A minute ago, Peter had been wishing she'd give *him* a massage. Not anymore.

"Start moving the plants," Nathan said.

"I think you're telling me I've got no charm. I'm hurt."

His friend guffawed.

"You didn't answer my question." Jasmine glanced over. "Do you like her? Because she's never going to believe you want to date her if there isn't some chemistry going on."

Was he attracted to her? Peter twisted his jaw to one side as he contemplated. "I don't know. We kind of got off on the wrong foot. She went all Ms. Attorney on me in like two seconds flat. It's hard to know what it might have been like if I'd met her under different circumstances."

Nathan gave a low whistle.

Peter scowled at his friend. "What's that supposed to mean?"

"He means you're not denying it, which is rather unusual." Jasmine pressed a kiss to Nathan's hair.

"Would you stop with the PDA already? Maybe it's your fault, with all your public displays of affection reminding me of what I don't have."

Nathan pulled Jasmine around and into his lap. "Is that so?"

"Seriously. Can we come to a plan of action about the house? Tell me what's wrong with my idea."

Jasmine slipped her arms around her husband's neck, snuggling against him. "Do you want to kiss her?" She watched Peter as she nibbled Nathan's ear.

"Ew, stop it. No, of course not. I met her once, for like twenty minutes, tops. I definitely did not stand there dreaming about kissing her."

"Instead, you had asparagus on the brain." Nathan nuzzled Jasmine's throat.

"Oh, good grief. Someone has to think about Bridgeview Backyards. You two are obviously not worried about business. You're not living with Alex and trying to get your life together enough to quit your job. Seems like it's all up to me."

Jasmine giggled and slid off Nathan's lap. "It's not like we're living in our dream house either."

"No, but you own it free and clear, thanks to Nathan's dad. Not that you wished he'd die or anything. I get that. But it doesn't change the fact that you have a home, that Nathan's built a solid reputation as a consultant here in just one year, and that you—" he pointed at Jasmine "—are able to work *our* business full-time while I'm still stuck working for the State. I'd think you'd care a little more."

"We also inherited a teenager," Jasmine reminded him. "Raising a half-brother isn't exactly the fast track to marital bliss."

Peter relaxed slightly. At least his cousin and business partner was finally talking seriously. "If you think mine is a bad idea, I'd like to hear yours."

"I'm fresh out." She shook her head. "I agree with Nathan. It's time to accept the loss and start moving plants. We've already planted everything we can over here. Our neighbors have too many trees, and the soil is too rocky for asparagus. How about down by the permaculture forest? Do you think Wade and Rebekah would mind?"

Peter grimaced. "People are too accustomed to helping themselves to whatever's on that lot. It's public. They wouldn't understand that some of it is for selling for profit."

"No, you're right." She angled her head and looked up at him. "You keep not telling me what our new attorney friend looks like. If you're going to be dating her, I'd like to know. Maybe I should go meet her."

"She's three, maybe four, inches shorter than me. Pretty enough." He waved his hands in a slight hour-glass shape. "A little heavy, maybe. Not that looks are everything."

"Sounds like you're over-protesting."

Was he? The only reason Sadie Guthrie was stuck in his head was because she was living in the house he'd counted on buying, denying him access to the yard he'd counted on gardening in. It wasn't because she was pretty or because he was attracted to her or because of her enticing vanilla scent or because her hair had soft curls or for any other reason.

Peter shook his head. "Everyone else I know, like my parents, is already using their yards to full capacity. I don't imagine we could convince Nonna."

Jasmine let loose a laugh. "Oh, nice try, Peter. She's going to be gardening that yard of hers until the day she dies. She might need help and she might complain how her joints ache, but she won't give up control. You know that."

"Have you asked her? I doubt she'll give in to me, though we all know I'm her favorite grandson, but maybe you? You've got a special bond with her, since there aren't that many girls." His own younger sisters found Nonna difficult and didn't put in much effort. Jasmine, though...

"I don't know. I don't think it's the best solution, honestly. She may deny it, but she's getting on. While her executor won't swoop in from out of state and sell the place to a stranger the way Beulah Essery's son did, I'm not sure who will inherit Nonna's house." Jasmine's shoulders slumped. "I don't want to imagine a life without her, but we have to be realistic. It's coming, and I don't think tying up her space for Bridgeview Backyards is wise."

"You're probably right." Peter didn't want to think about losing his grandmother, either. She was an opinionated old lady who ruled the neighborhood as though she were royalty but, beneath her crusty exterior, she was a woman who loved her God and her family with equal passion.

He grabbed his baseball cap from the doorknob. "Guess I'm the only one with a plan, then." He poked his chin toward Nathan. "Three-on-three tonight? Got a few guys lined up. It's only ten weeks until Hoopfest, and we need all the practice we can get."

Nathan tugged Jasmine back into his lap. "Not tonight."

Jasmine smirked.

Peter was so out of there.

CHAPTER 4

*T*he elevator doors slid open on the eleventh floor, and Sadie stepped out into the domain of Dawson and Banks Family Law. Her heels clicked on the hard floor, and Hazel glanced up from behind the chrome and glass desk.

"Good morning, Sadie. It's good to have you back. Are you all settled in?"

Sadie smiled at the older woman who'd been a fixture in the office forever. "I think it takes longer than a week to settle in, exactly, but I made a good start, and Anastasia has found a few favorite spots to sleep in the sun and watch the neighborhood."

"Cats." Hazel chuckled. "I hope you're ready to get right back into the swing of things. Mr. Banks wants to see you immediately."

Of course, he did. With Hugh Banks, everything was urgent. Sadie had panicked the first few times she'd received a summons like this one, but he'd never raked her over the coals yet, so her nerves had finally subsided. "Certainly. Is he with someone now, or shall I go right in?" She glanced toward his office, where the door stood slightly ajar.

"He's expecting you."

"Thanks, Hazel." Sadie shifted her briefcase into her other hand, crossed the expanse of marble, and tapped lightly on Hugh's door.

"Sadie? Come on in."

"Good morning, Hugh. Hazel said you wanted to see me."

He waved her to a seat and leaned back in his own, the Spokane skyline obscured in the gray drizzle behind him. Guess Peter Santoro wouldn't be gardening today.

"Yes. I needed to remind you that the fundraiser for the homeless is fast approaching. Hazel has a pair of tickets for you. Have you given any thought to who might be your plus-one?"

Sadie's brain froze. She might consider Jesus and Anastasia to be her roommates, but neither was a suitable plus-one for a formal event. "The date again?"

"May first."

She nodded slowly. How pathetic was it that her first thought was that Stan wouldn't be in Spokane that week? He'd arranged a whirlwind of viewings with a real estate agent — not Garry Bertoli, thankfully — for this coming week but then would return to Cannon Beach to list his house there. Did she actually want her adoptive father as her escort? Absolutely not, but he was the only man in her life.

Yes, pathetic.

Sadie shifted in the uncomfortable chair. "I'm sure no one will notice or care if I'm there alone."

"Ms. Guthrie." Hugh frowned at her over the rims of his glasses.

She took a deep breath. "Yes, sir?"

"People will absolutely notice, but it's more than that. You work hard, but you need someone in your life for your sake as well as for the event. Consider this your assignment on a personal level. I'm not asking you to be married or even engaged in the next month, and I know your opinion of cohabitation. But, please... look around you, find some young man who seems nice, and get to know him. There could be some trial and error. I get that. But put in an effort." He tapped his pen against the glass desk. "And, please, bring someone to the fundraiser."

How weird was it that the second man who came to mind was her backyard intruder? Wow, Hugh was right. She really needed to get out more. "I'll take that into consideration. Was there anything else?"

"You've got a dossier on your desk for a new case. I'll let you look it over." He glanced at the clock. "I have a client in five minutes, but check with me later if you have any questions."

Sadie rose, clutching her briefcase. "Thank you, sir."

The new case sounded much more alluring than lining up a date for an event that was still three weeks in the future, but she couldn't help running through a mental list of the single men in her current church. Dating. Dating. Newly engaged. Too awkward. Too weird. Dating.

Did she plan to keep attending there, even after moving halfway across the city? The teaching was okay. The setting somewhat formal, but she hadn't made any real friends. Not even girlfriends, let alone guys. Of course, only a loser guy would look twice at a fat girl like her. She didn't want a loser guy. She wanted a smart man who was easy on the eyes.

Maybe she should join a gym, but the thought of working out in public gave her palpitations. Okay, working out anywhere. She had a house now. One of the bedrooms could be a home gym, right? Not that having one more reason to hibernate would get her out meeting people.

Oh, who was she kidding? Any equipment she might buy would only collect dust and laundry.

And any man she looked twice at wouldn't be looking back.

Peter Santoro was a fine specimen. Too bad they'd gotten off on the wrong foot. She'd seen him hop into a truck with Washington State Fish and Wildlife emblazoned on the door several times, so he had a decent job. Probably a degree.

But, yeah. He disliked her as much as she disliked him. And there were tiny shoots of green coming up in neat rows beside her back fence. He hadn't ripped them out. It probably didn't hurt anything to leave them for now, until the landscaper showed up to do his thing. She could do that. A peace offering, of sorts.

Sadie slid behind her desk, opened the new folder, and scanned the contents. Sadly, a woman filing for divorce wasn't unusual, but the couple's minor children had been adopted from the state's foster care system. Hadn't those poor kids gone through enough? They were old enough to remember life before stability, and now their world was being rocked again.

This couple needed counseling, not a divorce. They needed to stay together for the sake of their children. Oh.

Except Ms. Halburton claimed her estranged husband was an adulterer.

Still. Counseling. Prayer. Surely there was a way to keep this family together. Think of those kids.

Stan and Lynda may have had difficulty showing love to their adoptive daughter — or each other, for that matter — but at least they'd stuck it out.

The Halburton children deserved that much.

⌐ ⌐ ⌐

"Thanks for inviting me for supper." Peter toed off his muddy boots in the Ropers' entryway. "I'd have turned you down if it wasn't pouring buckets out there. Too much to do in the gardens."

Rebekah laughed. "Wade knows better than to invite you when the weather's good. We haven't seen you for a while except around church."

"Not entirely true." Wade chuckled. "I see Santoro most days at work. One of us is always coming or going. But socially? Miss you, man." He punched Peter's arm.

"I'd hoped to submit my resignation to Fish and Wildlife by now, so you're lucky to see me at all."

Rebekah's grin faded. "Have you heard from your cousin?"

Peter didn't need to ask which of his many cousins. He hung his coat and followed Wade and Rebekah past the end of the staircase and into the living room. "My uncle and aunt hear from Basil just often enough to know he's still alive. He's waiting tables at the Fireweed. I guess it's an upscale restaurant in Seattle, so he's making good tips."

Wade shook his head. "I can't imagine Basil waiting tables."

"Oh, I don't know," said Rebekah. "He can pour on the charm when he wants to. I imagine he'd do that for a paycheck."

"Is he in addiction counseling?" Wade wanted to know.

"I think so. Sounds like he's doing okay, but with no desire to return to Spokane." If Peter had messed up as badly as his cousin had, he wouldn't want to show his face around Nonna, either. Basil's misstep dating Dixie Wayling — who was living with Dan Ranta and had just had his baby — the drunk driving, the jail time... Basil Santoro had not been a model citizen.

Peter worried about his cousin having cut ties, though. If the guy had found it so easy to slip into destructive patterns in the bosom of the Santoro family, how much simpler when there was no one around with a vested interest in him?

Then there was the fact that Basil had been one of the threesome who'd started Bridgeview Backyards, along with his sister and Peter. He'd had no savings to fall back on after his trial, leaving the other two to scrape together funds to buy him out.

Even if Peter wanted to make amends with his cousin, he couldn't very well quit his job *and* close their business to move to Seattle, just so Basil could avoid him there, too.

"Peetah!" Olivia, Wade and Rebekah's toddler, careened into the room dragging a ratty blanket. She careened toward Peter but veered off before he could scoop her up and give her a whisker rub.

Peter chuckled. "Why do I always get the impression she'd like to stuff this *pita* with falafel and take a bite?"

"Hey, she remembers you. It's not everyone she'll call by name." Wade picked up the tiny girl and swung her to his hip as he turned to the kitchen. "Let's go help Mama, Livvie."

"He'p!"

Peter followed the little family into the kitchen, where Rebekah bent over the open oven.

"Let me get that." Wade set Olivia down then reached inside for the large roasting pan. "Be careful lifting things, woman. Take care of that baby."

"I'm not fragile," Rebekah protested as she stepped out of his way, her round belly reminding Peter his friends were soon due with their second child.

Which only served to remind him that he was single with no end in sight. Reminding himself he was in no hurry had lost its calming influence in the past year or two.

Wade lifted the lid, and the aroma of pot roast and vegetables swirled around the room.

Peter's gut rumbled in anticipation. "Smells awesome. One of my favorite meals. What can I do to help?"

"Set the table?" suggested Rebekah. "Olivia likes to help with the cutlery."

Wade transferred the meat to a cutting board as Peter lifted plates from the cupboard. He'd been a regular in this house ever since Wade bought it nearly four years earlier, before his marriage to Rebekah. Peter had helped sand and refinish floors, paint walls, and wrangle new appliances into place. He certainly knew where the plates were kept.

He began filling glasses from the fridge dispenser then felt Olivia tugging on his jeans. "Wawa?"

"Can you fill her sippy cup, too?" asked Rebekah. "It's right there on the ledge."

"Got it." He filled the plastic cup and snapped the spouted lid in place before handing it to the little one.

She toddled off and stretched to put it on the edge of the table.

Every time he spent time around her, Peter's mind turned to mush. Same thing happened with his nine-month-old nephew, Gavin, who was a happy-go-lucky speed-crawler. Peter's mom watched her grandson every day so Dafne could finish up her senior year of high school. Not the ideal way to start a family. Peter understood that more than most after watching his teen sister's struggles and tears. One of these days Jasmine and Nathan were going to announce a pregnancy. He could sense the signs, even as he cringed at the thought of his business partner unable to put in the long hours needed for growing Bridgeview Backyards. Another pair of friends — Adriana and Myles Sheridan — were due in fall.

When was it ever going to happen for Peter? Every time he saw his grandmother, she asked him to hurry up and get her some more great-grandbabies. He was ready to meet the woman of his dreams any day now.

Peter hoisted Olivia into her booster seat and buckled her in as Rebekah brought the bowl of aromatic roasted veggies. He sniffed appreciatively. "What's all in there? Carrots, onions, celery, potatoes..."

Rebekah set the pottery bowl on the table and glanced at him. "Are you a picky eater, Peter?"

"Me? No. I'll eat anything that holds still."

"Okay, then I'll tell you about my experiment." She lowered her voice and turned away from the kitchen where Wade plated thick slices of roast beef. "I've heard roasted radishes are indistinguishable from potatoes. My obstetrician is concerned about my blood sugar — something about bordering on gestational diabetes — and advised me to eat fewer high-glycemic carbs, like potatoes, pasta, and bread. And any sweets, of course." She shook her head and sighed. "Not good news for a mama who's craving everything. I'm not convinced about radishes, but I'll try nearly anything once. I even tossed in a cut-up turnip."

Peter took a closer look at the veggies. "You're telling me there are no potatoes? Those sure look like halves of baby reds."

"Not one potato was sliced or diced in the making of this meal. I probably shouldn't have told you until after we'd eaten. Now you'll be prejudiced against them, like I am."

"Not at all. I'm curious. I'm a meat and potatoes guy myself, but the idea of subbing radishes intrigues me. I imagine there will be a peppery flavor."

"The low-carb websites say radishes lose all bite when cooked. But I guess we'll be the judges of that."

Wade set the platter of sliced meat on the table as Olivia banged her sippy cup. "Ready? Let's have a seat, give thanks, and dig in."

After Wade's prayer, Peter helped himself to a large scoop of roasted vegetables. He ground a little salt on top but left the pepper. Surely the radishes would provide plenty of that in every bite. He chewed what had to be a radish. The flavor wasn't identical to a potato, but he wasn't sure he'd have noticed if Rebekah hadn't warned him. He met her gaze. "That's not bad, actually."

"You're supposed to rave over my wife's cooking more than that." Wade cut meat into tiny pieces and set them in front of Olivia.

Peter grinned. "Great meal. Thanks for the invite, Rebekah. Just what I needed. A night away from Alex and the weight of trying to figure out how to handle the loss of the yard next door. I wish I knew what to do about it."

His friends glanced at each other. "Give us the details," suggested Rebekah. "We can pray with you for a solution."

Peter caught them up to date while they ate, including the fact that he hadn't made any moves to dig up the raspberry canes or asparagus roots yet. The endless drizzle was against him.

"I only see one solution." Wade leaned back in his chair and patted his full stomach.

Peter's spirits rose in anticipation. "Oh?"

"I think you'll have to marry the woman."

Rebekah giggled. "Is that an option, Peter?"

It didn't help that he wasn't the only person who'd concluded that was the only answer. And yet, Peter believed in real marriage, the kind where a couple both loved God and adored each other. A sham marriage to gain access to the property he wanted was not anything that he'd ever actually consider. It was just a joke.

It really was.

Wasn't it?

CHAPTER 5

A tall, lanky guy in ratty jeans and a ball cap stood at Sadie's door, staring out at her backyard.

She hesitated a moment. She'd glanced at Ranta Land-scaping's website, noticed a Water Street address and an 'established 1989' logo, and assumed she'd be dealing with an older man. Either way, she couldn't very well leave him standing out there in the dreary April weather. She opened the door and stepped outside, wrapping her sweater tighter around her at the chill. "Hi, you must be Dan Ranta. I'm Sadie Guthrie."

He looked down at her and stuck out his hand. "Yes, I'm Dan. Pleased to meet you. This is the yard in question?"

"Um... yes?" What other yard would she have called regarding a quote?

"I hadn't heard that Mrs. Essery sold out."

"Actually, she passed away about a month ago now."

"I see." He pursed his lips. "This is one of Bridgeview Backyards' leased properties, isn't it?"

"Bridgeview Backyards?"

Dan motioned to the house next door. "Peter Santoro. Jasmine Sant — I mean, Jasmine Hamelin. The business they run."

"Peter. I've met him." But business? What was this guy talking about?

"Didn't he tell you? I thought he was going to buy this place."

Sadie pushed out a laugh and huddled into her sweater. "He thought so, too, from what I gathered. Nevertheless, I bought the property from the estate. Private sale."

"That's too bad."

"I'm not sure what you mean. I called you to get a quote on redoing this into a backyard oasis, not to get a lecture about a random guy's dream to dig the whole thing up for vegetables."

He looked at her again. "They're doing good things with their business. Offering subscriptions so people can get boxes of fresh vegetables delivered once a week for the entire growing season."

"I'm happy for them." Although finding out it was a business — obviously a sideline considering the Fish and Wildlife truck — did put a slightly different spin on it. Maybe the guy didn't live off tons of vegetables. "But it has no bearing on my plans. I'd like a vibrant flowerbed along that fence." She motioned toward the rows of short green plants. "A selection that will bloom for as long as possible, that smells good and attracts butterflies."

"Any particular species of plants?"

"Roses?" She shrugged. "I honestly don't know. You're the expert. Give me ideas. The trees on the west side can stay if they're healthy, since they offer good evening shade.

Then this area here I'd like paved with bricks or something that suits the era of the house. A pond or fountain, maybe both. And some kind of shade or rain structure that can be retracted. I anticipate spending a lot of time back here, unwinding from a stressful job, and I don't want the weather interfering."

Dan nodded as though she'd made a reasonable request. "Budget?"

Always the kicker. "I'd like to see two or three options at different price-points, but I do have funds set aside for this project." The interior could wait if needed.

"I'll get you a couple of quotes in May."

"Um... I was hoping to get started before then." Like this weekend.

"Sorry, ma'am. Ranta Landscaping is in high demand. My sister does most of the designing — she's taking horticulture at a college in Edmonds — so I'll put her on this as soon as she's back in Spokane for the summer. Her husband is our master craftsman. You don't want anyone but Logan building that shade structure. We can probably have everything finished by September."

She swung to face him, but the guy didn't look like he was kidding. "That long?" Why wasn't instant gratification a thing?

"Sorry. You're welcome to see if my competition is available sooner, but I'll leave you with one question. Do you want to trust someone with no projects lined up, or do you want to trust someone whose work is in demand, even if it means waiting for an opening?"

"Well, when you put it that way..."

He nodded, still not smiling. "Trust me. We're worth

waiting for, and I can give you references if you like. Once you have the quotes, don't wait too long to decide. Our schedule is filling up quickly."

She'd checked the testimonials on their website already. "I'd like to see what your sister comes up with."

Dan reached up and tugged the brim of his baseball cap. "You won't be sorry."

That was his left hand. He wore no ring. Was he single? Both Hugh and Cordell had reminded her every day this week to be seeking a plus-one for the fundraiser. Man, she hated looking like a desperate woman. But that didn't miti-gate the facts.

"Dan, I've got an unrelated question."

He turned back toward her. "Yes?"

Sadie took a deep breath and let the words tumble out. "I can't help noticing you're not wearing a wedding ring, and usually that means a guy is single. If you're single and not busy on the night of May first, I need a date to a fundraiser event for Blessings Under the Bridge, and I wondered if you might be interested."

His eyes narrowed slightly.

Not a good sign.

"Not married, but not available either. Good luck finding someone." He shook his head as he jogged down the steps and rounded the corner of the house.

Well. That hadn't been awkward at all.

⌒ ⌣ ⌣

LIVING in Bridgeview was going to be the death of her. Why had she thought an evening stroll might be a good idea, just because the sky had brightened just enough for a gorgeous rainbow in the eastern sky? One glance through the window before heading out should have reminded her that any time a person could see across the roofs of nearby houses, it meant the hillside was steep. So steep that many of the streets didn't go all the way through, but staircases connected one level to another between the precipitous roadways.

No way was she making it all the way down to the riverfront path without driving. Just thinking about hiking back up the one block she'd just walked down was more than enough.

She usually drove the most direct route to her downtown office, so tonight was for getting a glimpse of her immediate neighborhood. The bridge loomed just over her right shoulder as it headed for the north shore with Bridgeview and the river below. Across the street stood a large brick building with a sign stating it was the community center. Nice. She'd be on the lookout for events happening there... but would they welcome a newcomer?

"And one!" yelled a male voice.

Sadie scanned the area and saw a basketball court beneath the bridge itself where half a dozen guys in shorts and tees bounced a brown ball around. Weren't they freezing? It had rained for the better part of a week, and the air was still chilly.

"Go, Alex!"

Alex? Wasn't that the name of her other next-door neighbor? The one she'd seen wearing a suit and tie driving out in an older model car? If Alex were here, that meant...

A player jumped, and the ball swished through the hoop. "Peter's the man!" one of the guys called out.

Peter was here.

And she really shouldn't stare. Honestly, she was watching all of them. Six guys with sweat pouring off their faces by the way they wiped them on their T-shirts between intense bouts of play. They ducked under each other's elbows, dodged, bounced the ball, leaped, and threw. Thump. Thump. Swish.

Laughing. Hand-slapping. Shoulder-punching. Part of something. Maybe a family, since she recalled Peter and Alex were cousins, but more than relatives. Friends. Buddies. Chums.

Sadie had spent her entire life standing on the outside looking in. Stan and Lynda were both only children and had rarely returned to Illinois to visit their families after their move to Oregon. Lynda's mom had visited two or three times.

This whole business of a bunch of relatives living near each other was completely foreign. Imagine having cousins who doubled as friends. Never mind that. Start with having siblings or cousins at all.

She'd facilitated an international adoption for a single woman and a small boy from the Dominican Republic, and it had made her think about doing the same thing. She made good money and, now that she had a home, she could share her resources and affection with a child in need. After all, she was unlikely to ever marry. She was Stan's only heir. Who would be hers?

And yet, didn't a kid deserve two parents? Maybe a couple of brothers or sisters?

Sadie tugged her coat tighter, huddling against the chilly wind as the clouds shifted back in. This was crazy. All she'd wanted was to get outside for a few minutes and see a bit of her neighborhood, and instead she was staring at a bunch of guys playing basketball and wishing she had a sibling.

She pivoted and took a few steps up the sidewalk. Her thighs were going to die before she made it up this steep block.

"Sadie!"

No. She'd been spotted. Should she turn back? Wouldn't it be rude if she didn't? She wanted to be part of this community, a place that actually had a building they called its center.

"Sadie! Hey, come meet the guys."

She didn't want to meet the guys. Or did she? It didn't matter. She couldn't pretend not to have heard. She turned to see Peter jogging toward her, mopping his face on a gray towel slung over his shoulder. A guy with tousled hair and sweat stains on his blue T-shirt should not look this attractive. But his grin looked as real as his track shorts and white tennis shoes. "Hey, guys. This is Sadie, who bought Mrs. Essery's house."

Sadie waited for the bitterness to seep from his voice. For the men gathered to scowl at the introduction. Neither happened.

"Have you met Alex?"

She shook her head, though she knew which he was. "Pleased to meet you."

He grinned. "Likewise."

"This is Nathan, my cousin-in-law."

That was a thing? Sadie smiled and nodded.

"Alex's brothers Marco and Evan, and Nathan's brother Jason."

Sadie pulled her hand from her deep pocket for a little wave. "Hi."

Peter jiggled the ball. "Want to play?"

"Yeah, come on."

Which guy had that been? And didn't any of them have eyes? She wasn't dressed for it. She was fat, not fit. "No, thanks." She shook her head.

"Some other time, maybe," Peter suggested, flicking the ball at a younger guy who caught it even though there'd been no eye contact or warning.

"I don't play." Seriously, wasn't it obvious?

Alex chuckled. "It's what we do in Bridgeview."

Sadie's eyebrows rose. "Looks like a guy thing."

"Tonight, it is. My sister is pretty good, though. So are some of the other females around. You just happened to catch us on Testosterone Night."

Peter tipped his head back and laughed, a full, rich sound. "Truth be told, women are always welcome, but they don't usually come. Seriously, if you want to play anytime, you're welcome. Everyone's a beginner when they start."

He was missing the part where she was uninterested, not to mention overweight. "Thanks." She took a step backward. "Don't let me keep you from your game. Have fun." Another step back, then suddenly she was toppling, her arms flailing to keep her balance, her behind landing hard on the pavement, her head jolting back and colliding just as hard.

Why hadn't she remembered the curb? And now she

was flat on her back with a cracked skull and six sweaty guys reaching for her arms to help her up.

She wasn't cold anymore. Her face was so flushed she felt the blaze through her entire body. Why did these things always happen to her? She was so clumsy, so inept, so unathletic. So chubby.

The guys hoisted her upright then stepped back. Peter looked concerned, bless him. "You okay? That was quite a fall."

"Missed the curb," she mumbled. "I'll be fine."

"You sure? I'd better walk you home."

"No, really." But the pounding in her head only intensified as she reached to feel the back of her skull. At least her hand didn't come away covered in blood. She'd probably have fainted and collapsed again.

"You guys go ahead. I'll be back in a few." Peter took her arm.

She could feel the heat of his hand even through her sweater and coat.

"It's fine. I need to get home and help put the boys to bed," one of the other men said.

"I've got an exam tomorrow," said another. "Gotta study some more."

"Yeah, it was fun. Let's do it again soon."

Great. Her clumsiness had broken up their game. She looked at Peter. "I'm okay, really." With any luck, this was nothing a bubble bath and a few painkillers wouldn't cure.

His blue eyes stared intensely back at her. "You can't get rid of me that easily."

Was he talking about more than a walk up the hill?

CHAPTER 6

*H*er breath came in short, sharp puffs after only a dozen steps. Was she hurting from her fall, or just winded? He'd grown up active, running, climbing, playing sports. Taken it for granted.

Peter glanced at the woman beside him. Didn't look like she'd had a similar upbringing. Why had he asked her to join them? Clearly, she wasn't dressed for sports, not in dressy shoes and navy slacks beneath a long navy coat. And, yeah, she was a little... round... but that didn't mean anything. His cousin Fran was a bit heavier than many women he knew, and she had no trouble holding her own in three-on-three. Come to think of it, Fran hadn't joined them recently.

Sadie paused and closed her eyes, her chest heaving. She'd already pulled away from him and jammed both hands in her coat's deep pockets.

"You okay?" Dumb question, since she obviously wasn't, but he didn't know what else to say.

"I'll live." Her eyes fluttered open — long eyelashes,

wow — and she looked up the block. "I didn't realize... how steep everything is... in this neighborhood."

Peter bit his tongue against commenting that it really wasn't that vertical. To her, it obviously was. "You'll get used to it."

"Maybe." She gaze still angled up toward Wilson Avenue. "Or maybe I'll be smart enough to drive everywhere from now on."

He grinned. "That's not smartness. That's..."

Her carefully plucked eyebrows rose as she looked at him. "Laziness?"

Peter held up both hands and kept the grin in place. "Not what I was going to say at all." His brain scrambled for a different word.

"You don't have to lie."

No forgetting she was perceptive and blunt. Must be the attorney in her. "I meant it when I said you'll get used to it. People in Bridgeview tend to walk a lot. It's often faster than driving all the way around. Plus, when you're walking, you have a chance to stop and chat with neighbors and friends as they're puttering in their yards."

She started up the hill. "I haven't seen any sign that you're moving plants out of mine."

He'd opened himself up for that. "It's done not much else but rain since we had our little talk."

"I imagine it wouldn't be all that pleasant to work in."

"That's part of it, but tromping on and digging in wet soil will only compact it. You'll be left with packed earth that much harder to work with."

Sadie's breathing sharpened as they ambled past the house beside the community center. "It doesn't matter."

"Well, yes, it does, because you'll want to grow something there yourself."

"That's not what I meant." She halted again, and Peter stopped beside her. "I meant I've talked to three landscaping contractors and none of them can do anything for several months. I had no idea it would take so long."

Peter's heart pounded a little harder. "What are you saying?"

"You've got until the end of July to get your plants out of there. It's not like I'll be able to make my plans happen before then, anyway. And I certainly don't want to be digging around in the dirt on my own."

"It's therapeutic."

"Sure, it is. For some people. My work demands long hours. It's very stressful, and I'd like to spend what I have actually relaxing."

"Everyone needs hobbies." He grinned to take the sting out of his words. "What's yours?"

"Reading." She trudged forward once again.

"Cool. I often plug in a science fiction audiobook while I'm gardening. What's your favorite genre?"

She didn't reply.

Peter wished he'd brought a jacket himself. He'd have been home five minutes ago if he hadn't offered to walk with Sadie. Only to make sure she made it okay, of course, after that clunk to her head.

"Oh, being one with nature isn't quite enough?"

"My cousin and I run a backyard gardening business in five yards, including our own. She's full-time through the season, but I'm still holding down a day job as well."

"One of the contractors I interviewed mentioned something about your business."

"Must've been Dan Ranta."

"Yes. Yes, it was."

"Good guy."

"He seemed nice." Her face flushed.

If they walked any slower, a caterpillar would win the race. "Dan's one of the best in the city for environmental practices. You'll be pleased with the results." Peter glanced down at the top of Sadie's springy curls. Why not take a chance? "Unless you decide to sign your own agreement with Bridgeview Backyards, in which case Jasmine and I will handle everything. We can work around your plans for a patio and arbor." It'd cut down on additional growing space but leave the berries and asparagus intact. He could live with a compromise.

"In your dreams."

Well, yes. Definitely.

"Just be thankful I'm not forcing the issue this week, all right? It would be entirely within my rights to do so."

"Now you're talking like a lawyer again."

Her chin came up. "I *am* one."

Peter needed to remember she wasn't tease-able like his sisters and cousins. "What kind of law?"

"Family."

Hmm. "Sounds more fun than clapping criminals behind bars."

"I've done a bit of that."

Interesting. He'd need to look into family law and see what it covered, just to satisfy his curiosity. His mind drifted to his kid sister raising a baby without any help from the father. "Some families need all the help they can get."

"They do."

They finally reached the intersection of their own street, which meant his time with Sadie would soon end. Why did that disappoint him? Maybe he wasn't all talk about asking her out. He managed to cover his reactionary snort with a pretend sneeze.

She glanced up at him. "Coming down with a cold?"

"I don't think so." He grinned at her. "No time for nonsense like that."

Sadie studied his face for a moment. "You mentioned families needing help."

Uh... where was she going with this? "Yes?"

"There's a fundraiser event coming up on May first for Blessings Under the Bridge, and my firm, Dawson and Banks, is one of the sponsors. My boss insists I attend with a plus-one. Might you be interested?"

Peter angled his head to one side and tried to meet her gaze, but her eyes wouldn't quite connect. "You're asking me out."

If she turned any redder she'd put a radish to shame. "It's to raise money for food and other necessities for the homeless. That's all. Not like a date. Not really."

He grinned. "You *are* asking me out."

"For a good cause."

He'd never seen this coming. "May first, you said?"

She peeked at him through those long, thick lashes. "Yes?"

"I'll double check my calendar, but I think I'm free. Pray for rain."

"For rain?"

"Yes, otherwise I should probably be out in the garden. Spring is a busy time of year for Bridgeview Backyards." As was summer. And definitely fall.

"Okay, I'll pray for rain. It's a formal event. You'll need to wear a tuxedo or a nice suit."

She'd be in a gown, then. What color and style would she favor? He could hardly wait to see. "I own a tux. With so many cousins, it seemed cheaper to buy one than keep renting for weddings."

Sadie blinked. "Well, that's good."

"I'll need your cell phone number."

"You will?"

His grin widened. "To confirm the *date*." He placed extra emphasis on the word and felt a surge of satisfaction at her blush.

⌒ ℓ ℓ

"*YOU ASKED HIM OUT?*"

Sadie held her cell phone at arm's length while Denae squealed from her home in Missoula. When the giggles toned down, she put the device back to her ear. "Because my bosses wouldn't let up. That's all. So, get the idea of romance out of your head."

"I'll never get romance out of my head, silly."

That sentiment probably came from Denae's career as a sought-after editor for both traditional and indie-published authors of romance and romantic suspense. If anyone lived, breathed, and practically *bathed* in romance, it was Sadie's best friend.

"And here you thought he was a serial killer," she teased as Anastasia leaped onto her lap. The Siamese kneaded Sadie's thigh then curled into a tight ball.

"I was editing a particularly creepy suspense story that week," Denae responded. "I'm glad to know he's just an ordinary guy. But you did say hunky, didn't you?"

"I'm sure I didn't." Even though Peter Santoro was all that and more, Sadie distinctly remembered not describing him to Denae as she watched him through the window.

"What are you going to wear? And don't tell me that blue dress you bought four years ago. It's tired and out of style."

Here's not where she told her uber-skinny friend that the blue dress was too tight, anyway. She'd tried it on last night, and it wouldn't zip up. Apparently, she either needed to lose five pounds before May first, buy shapewear, or splurge on a new dress. Maybe all three. "I'm going shopping, I guess. Can you make a trip out? You know I hate buying clothes."

"Ooh. Let me check my day planner." Paper rustled. "Aargh. It looks like back-to-back projects for the next six weeks."

The idea wouldn't let go. "I've got internet and a spare room. Furnished, even. You can work from here, can't you? And just take a few hours off to go shopping?" Although finding a gown that looked halfway decent could take days. Sadie's gut sank. Why had she let Hugh Banks talk her into this? But, as she recalled the conversation, he hadn't left her an option. She was attending. As it turned out, she'd be attending on the arm of a very handsome, eligible bachelor. One she'd threatened with legal action.

She winced, and Anastasia looked up, grumbling. *Sorry, cat.*

"I can't edit while I'm driving, and that's at least three hours each way if conditions are good. But, listen. I'll try to get ahead and see if I can't make it happen. You know me. I love to shop!"

Sadie did know. Sometimes she wondered how she and Denae had managed to become such good friends considering all the ways they were different. Denae's mom and stepdad lived in Cannon Beach, next door to Stan and Lynda, but Denae had spent a lot of time at her dad's ranch in Montana. Denae never seemed to be at a loss for friends. Maybe that was it. Her naturally bubbly personality gathered people around her, but she was so genuine that even Sadie had been pulled in and felt appreciated.

"I know you're busy, and I understand if you can't get away. The offer stands, though. Anytime you want to come, please do. You'll have plenty of work hours, because I put in tens at the office most days. Anastasia will enjoy the company, though I do generally have weekends off." And brought files home.

"You make it sound so enticing."

Sadie laughed. "It's my life. I chose it, so I can't complain."

"Bo-ring," teased Denae. Then she sobered. "Although I know what you do is very important. Kids need an advocate in this nasty world."

Her friend had felt shuffled between her parents. Only appreciated by her mom for the fact she was old enough to babysit her half-brothers and keep the house clean. No wonder she'd aligned with her dad after college. He was super busy, too, but at least he seemed to care, and Denae got along with his second wife.

What a mess families were.

Except maybe the Santoros. Hanging out with brothers and cousins was beyond Sadie's imagination, but then she'd never claimed to have a good one. Unlike Denae. "Hey, do you ever edit stories where everyone is related, and they really like each other?"

She could almost see Denae's slow blink. "Uh... in series, yes. What brought that on?"

"Peter. He lives with his cousin, who owns the house next door. Alex is an accountant or something like that. And Peter's in business with another cousin, Jasmine. The other night a bunch of them were playing basketball by the community center. He introduced me, and I think they were all cousins. It all seems... weird." Overwhelming.

"Cool. Yeah, I've edited series like that, so it's fun to know it can be true in real life as well. Not everyone has dysfunctional families like yours and mine, girlfriend."

Sadie let out a long breath. "Good thing."

"Too true. You said your dad is moving to Spokane? Maybe he's trying to do better."

"Maybe, but it's too little, too late."

"It's only too late when someone dies."

The stark reminder of Lynda's death hung in front of Sadie's mind. That day had crushed her completely. It hadn't been the woman's passing so much as Sadie's discovery she'd been adopted. The revelation had socked her so deeply in the gut, but it had definitely explained why she'd felt like an outsider all her life. "I get what you're saying, Denae, but he's not really my father."

Her friend sighed. "Sadie, he is. In every way that matters. He gave you his name; he gave you a home and opportunities most kids never get."

"What I needed was love."

"Don't we all? It's a basic human essential. Some authors I know use the hierarchy of need to help build characters."

Sadie had studied Maslow's theory in college. Everyone needed basic survival then safety then love in order to thrive. Stan and Lynda had supplied the first two, for sure. Food, water, air, shelter. A place of safety. They'd struggled with the third step, love and belonging, Oh, she had to admit that they'd tried, in their own way. Stan still made an attempt. After all, he'd uprooted his life to be near her.

What was Sadie supposed to do with that, when she'd already given up on feeling like she belonged? She'd forged ahead to the next level, seeking esteem. Respect always seemed fragile, but as she worked hard at Dawson and Banks, she'd gain that. She didn't need love anymore.

Part of her withered a bit at the thought. She did need love. More than her cat's love. More than her best friend's love. She still longed for a parent's love.

And maybe for the love of a significant other.

CHAPTER 7

*Y*ou can't be serious."

Peter waggled his eyebrows at his cousin. "And I didn't even need to do the asking. Women just can't resist me."

Jasmine let out an unladylike snort. "Which is precisely why you're twenty-eight and single."

He pressed a hand over his heart. "You wound me."

Nathan shook his head, grinning. They'd dropped by Alex's a few days after the three-on-three game. Everyone was eager to meet Logan and Linnea the minute they drove in from Seattle after months away at college.

"I'd even been looking at that event before Sadie invited me. I was going to talk to you about it, because it's just the sort of fundraiser I'd like Bridgeview Backyards to support. Then I looked at the price of the tickets and decided it wasn't in this year's budget."

"That steep, huh?" asked Nathan.

"Yes. And now my ticket is comped. Win, win."

"To say nothing of getting a date with the woman who holds your heart. I mean, your yard."

Peter gave Nathan two thumbs up. "And thaaat's not all."

"Said the radio announcer dramatically," Jasmine added, laughing.

"Well, yes. But the drama is necessary, because we can harvest our asparagus before she pulls out the garden. I won't push for the raspberries yet, but we might be able to get this year's crop of those as well."

Nathan's eyebrows peaked. "How so?"

"She figured she could call up a landscaper and they could start immediately. Now she knows the good ones are booked for months. In fact, our own Linnea Dermott will be designing Sadie's yard. If they ever get here."

Jasmine looked out the front window. "I'm so excited they'll be here for the summer, helping out with Bridgeview Backyards."

"Around working for Dan," Peter reminded her. "Linnea has several gardens to design, and Dan's contracting Logan for some gazebos and stuff. We only get their spare time."

"I'll take what we can get." Jasmine wrinkled her nose. "If only Basil—"

"Don't start, love," Nathan said conversationally. "Forget what might have been, and play with the cards we've been dealt."

She heaved a sigh. "I know. It's just he's such a moron."

"He's not a moron. He made some big mistakes, he's paying for them, and he's learning from them."

From where Peter sat, it sounded like Nathan had talked Jasmine through this dozens of times. Maybe he had. At least Jasmine wasn't quite as bitter toward her older brother as she had been last summer after his arrest.

"How's work these days?" Nathan asked.

Peter shrugged. "We're doing some controlled burns near the Idaho border while the ground is still wet. Same old, same old. You?"

"I've got a few new clients. Enough to keep me busy."

"That's good." Nathan's marketing genius had earned him a solid reputation throughout Spokane in the past year.

"They're here!" squealed Jasmine, dashing for the door.

Peter exchanged a chuckle with Nathan as they followed her through the carport to where Logan's car engine cut out. Linnea leaped from the passenger side and the two girls hugged each other fiercely. Logan took a few seconds longer to exit the driver's side. He embraced Nathan then Peter with a thump on their shoulders and stepped back.

"Nice to see you. Roads okay?" asked Nathan.

"No complaints." Logan stretched and looked around. "Wow, it's good to be home."

Peter nodded. "We're glad to have you two in the basement suite this summer. As you know, after Nathan got married and moved out, we rented to a student, but he's gone for a few months. This works out great for us. And by us, I mean Alex."

"Having an available rental here was the deciding factor for Linnea and me." Logan watched his wife. "One more year of college, and we'll be back for good."

"Diplomas in hand."

Logan grinned. "Yep. Ready to take on the world, one backyard at a time."

Peter glanced toward the house next door in time to see

the curtain shift in the front window. Either Sadie had been watching, or her cat was. He was trying to take over the world one backyard at a time, too... starting with the one next door.

Was it terrible of him to accept her invitation to the fundraiser? Did she think he was actually interested in her? Because he wasn't. It was all about protecting the garden.

"...Peter?"

He tuned back in as Logan mentioned his name. "Pardon me?"

Nathan chuckled. "Don't mind him. He's dreaming about the woman who bought Mrs. Essery's house. Young. Pretty. Single."

"A lawyer," added Peter, as though that explained everything else. It kind of did, after Evan informed them they didn't have a leg to stand on with their so-called agreements with the landowners.

Logan slugged his arm. "The mighty Pietro has fallen?"

Peter winced. "Only Nonna calls me that and gets away with it."

"Notice he's not denying it," Nathan said.

"You're living in a dream world," Peter informed him. "We're going out to a fundraiser."

Logan's eyebrows rose.

"Her boss pressured her for a plus-one. She asked me. You will notice no sign of romance in that transaction."

"Yo, is that really you talking about romance?" Linnea stepped up and gave him a quick hug before reaching for Nathan.

"Totally." Jasmine smirked. "He's feeling so lonely with everyone pairing off."

Peter rolled his eyes. "As if." It was kind of true, though. It wasn't just this bunch, but several of their other friends had married in the past year or two. Plenty of single guys remained, like Alex and Basil. Not that Basil still lived here. "Who's got time for that, with two jobs?"

"I managed," chimed in Jasmine. "Working with you and running the massage clinic while dating Nathan."

"And I notice you closed the clinic as soon as Nathan was able to support you. Some of us don't have that luxury, girl. There's no one to bail me out."

"Lawyers must make a mountain of money." Nathan thumbed over his shoulder at the house next door.

"You're hilarious." Peter draped an arm over Linnea's shoulder and began guiding her toward the house. "I want to talk to you about the yard design over there. Some requests."

"Oh?" She winked up at him. "I only take orders from the homeowner, so this can only mean you've got an inside scoop."

He groaned. "Find a way to save the asparagus patch if you can. That's all I ask. Losing that space is killing me."

"Enough to date her to get access?" She pulled away from him and planted her fists on her hips. "Because that is beneath you, Peter Santoro."

"It was a joke." Or, at least, it had started as one.

"But you're going out with her. Don't mess with a woman's emotions, buddy. I'm not kidding, even a little bit."

"Two separate issues. Honestly."

Linnea's eyebrows rose.

"Okay, I want the yard, and it crossed my mind and mouth to consider dating her for that reason." He held up both hands. "I know, I know. Bad Peter. But I wouldn't have done it, I promise. She's the one who invited me to an event I already wanted to attend. Should I have turned her down?"

"Watch your step. That's all I can say. Because I'm totally on her side in this, whatever side that is."

Peter winced. Yes, his motives hadn't been perfect when he'd considered dating Sadie, but he wouldn't actually have done anything about it. He'd been taught to consider all angles and possible solutions. This was one angle. A bad one, so he'd discarded it.

But the woman herself? She intrigued him, from the bristly first encounter to seeing her struggle with the hill to the fleeting hint of loneliness in her voice.

SADIE LOOKED from Denae's plate to hers in Frank's Diner. She pointed at the chef salad. "How will that ever keep you going until breakfast?"

"It's almost too much." Denae set the biscuit aside. "And I don't usually eat bread."

That probably accounted for why Sadie weighed twice as much. She should've known better than to order the chicken fried steak in front of her friend. The gravy was to die for, though, and almost made the asparagus drowning in it edible.

Denae had a nibble of her salad. "Are you happy with your dress?"

Sadie hesitated. "After I bought the tummy control underwear." Not that the foundation garment was a miracle worker. She'd need liposuction for that.

"The purple is gorgeous on you, and I love the matching heels we found."

"Thanks." Sadie couldn't help wondering why Denae never nagged at her about her weight. No matter how many openings Sadie gave her, her friend held back on criticism.

Denae pushed the food around her plate then finally set her fork aside. "I can't believe you actually asked the guy out. And enough with trying to tell me it was because your boss pushed you. He's asked you to bring a plus-one before and you never did."

"I've wondered myself what possessed me. I just don't do stuff like that."

Denae parked her elbows on the table and rested her chin on her joined hands. "He's awfully cute. Just the way I like 'em. Tall, dark, and handsome."

"He'd probably like you better than me."

"Uh uh." Her eyes grew wide as she shook her head. "I'm not stealing your man. And besides, why would he?"

"Well... you're thin. I'm not."

"Not all guys like thin. Besides, it doesn't matter. You're the one who asked him. You're the one he said yes to."

Sadie poked at her mashed potatoes. "I wonder why?"

"You told me he talked about families needing help. You obviously have something in common."

"You make it sound like you know all about it, and you're just as single as I am."

"But I've edited hundreds of romance novels, so I've learned a thing or two. You need something in common. You need a spark."

Was there a spark between her and Peter? Maybe, if she

could call their first meeting sparks instead of an explosion of TNT. He'd seemed pretty nice on the walk home, though. He hadn't made fun of her for being out of breath or being fat. He'd even teased her a little, like Denae might do. Like a friend.

"You need a situation that keeps pushing the two of you together." Denae tapped her fingers on the table "Living next door helps with that, and this fundraiser locks it in. Also, you need to share faith. Do you know if he's a believer?"

Sadie shook her head. "I told you, we've only spoken to each other two or three times."

"Okay, well, it's important you figure that out before you go much further. Next, you need conflict, because a relationship needs to be tested before you know it will hold up under pressure."

"Are you quite done? I'm not in one of your books."

Denae's eyebrows rose. "I've got a few more points to make."

"I don't want to hear them. We're going to a fundraiser for homeless people. This isn't exactly the stuff of romance."

"All bets are off when he sees you in that dress."

As if. That undergarment might help, but even a corset wouldn't get her anywhere near skinny. "I still think you should move to Spokane," Sadie blurted.

"I still think you should move to Montana," mimicked Denae.

"I'm not licensed to practice law there, but can't editors work from anywhere?"

Denae shrugged. "In theory, yes, but I'm not ready to

settle down, and I'm not a fan of cities. I know Spokane isn't huge, but it's way bigger than Missoula, and even that's too much for me. It's fun coming for some shopping and to see you, but that's about it."

"You're headed back tomorrow, then?"

"After church. Where do you attend?"

"I've been thinking about trying the neighborhood church over by the bistro. Bridgeview Bible. I'm not that attached to the one I attended near my old apartment."

"Sounds good. I'll come with you, then we'll do lunch before I hit the road."

Now she was committed, but maybe this was the push she'd needed. She hadn't gone anywhere since she'd moved, pretending she was busy unpacking. Which had sort of been true, but the excuse had run its course.

"Remind me to double check the website when we get back to the house, but I think it starts at ten-thirty."

"Still seems weird to have you living in my grandmother's house."

"Oh." Sadie had all but forgotten Denae's connection to the place. "I hope she'd be happy with what I'm doing to it."

Denae laughed. "I have a suspicion she'd rather have that hunky gardener working outside her window. Good eye candy even for an old lady."

And for a young one.

CHAPTER 8

*Y*ou were late for church," Wade whispered as he dug his elbow into Peter's side during the closing hymn.

Hard to deny. Peter had slipped in the back pew halfway through the singing. "I think it's ironic that Pastor Tomas preached on the Holy Spirit being like rain on the morning the hot water tank blew a pipe and gushed all over Alex's basement."

"No way!" Wade's eyes grew round as he shifted his sleeping toddler and rose to his feet. "Didn't Logan and Linnea just move in?"

"Thankfully they'd planned to unload the car this afternoon. All they'd brought in was an overnight bag. They might stay with Jacob and Eden for a day or two." Without hot water in the house, Peter was seriously considering bunking out at his parents' place for a bit. While he hated for it to be Alex's problem, the fact was... it was Alex's problem. Peter rented space, but Alex was the homeowner.

"Water's a good thing, in its place."

Peter laughed. "If you're still thinking of the sermon, that's like saying we should limit the Holy Spirit's access."

"Not what I meant." Wade sobered. "But we do like our compartments, don't we? God's great on Sunday morning and at regularly scheduled prayer time, but let's not get too crazy and let Him flood all areas of our lives."

"Radical thinking." Peter looked around the sanctuary of Bridgeview Bible Church. This was a different perspective. He normally sat closer to the front, not in the pews reserved for parents with small children. He watched as a bunch of his cousins and friends gathered around Logan and Linnea, welcoming them back for the summer months. Then he surveyed the rest of the thinning crowd, looking for his folks. He was headed to their place for lunch. They must already be out in the foyer.

His gaze nearly skipped over the two women but then swung back. Sadie and a friend? He'd barely gotten around to wondering about her spiritual status but seeing her in church was a good sign. Wait, had he threatened to sue another Christian that first day they'd met? As she chatted with the woman next to her, she turned and caught him staring.

Uh. Peter lifted a hand in acknowledgment and offered a small smile. Should he go talk to her? Introduce her to people? After all, they were going to the fundraiser together. It might seem like a date, but it wasn't. Not really. Not like two people who were attracted to each other. Still, looking at Sadie and her ultra-thin friend, he'd take a woman with a bit of padding any day. Her friend didn't even look healthy.

Great, now the skinny one had noticed his stare. He was

in for it now. Peter took a deep breath and wended his way toward them. "Good morning."

"Hi, Peter. I'd like you to meet Denae. Um... in person."

In person? Memory flooded back of the crazy voice on speaker phone. "Denae. Pleased to meet you. I didn't realize you lived in Spokane."

"I don't. I popped over from Missoula for the weekend to take Sadie shopping."

"That's... nice. Great."

"Her dress is purple."

Peter's eyebrows pulled together as he glanced back at Sadie. It looked blue to him. Closer to turquoise, really.

"Not this one, silly. The one she's wearing for the fundraiser."

That cleared things up. Sort of. He cleared his throat. "I'm sure it's a great color on her."

The thin woman's long black hair swung from side to side as she shook her head. "You don't get it, do you?"

Females. There might be more than one reason Peter was still single.

Denae sighed. "Men buy flowers for women when they go to a formal dinner. A wrist corsage would be lovely. I'm telling you the color, so you can order something that matches. Wild hyacinths are quite nice and would do the trick."

Sadie's face pinked.

Peter's might not be far behind. "Gotcha. Thanks for the tip." A tip Jasmine should have already mentioned, not that she was into formal events. Still, wasn't it her job to make sure Peter didn't look bad?

Sadie tucked her hand behind Denae's elbow. "We

should get going for lunch. Denae's headed back this afternoon."

"Safe travels. It was good to meet you." He turned back to Sadie. "And good to see you in church. I hadn't seen you here before." Would he ever feel like an idiot if she'd been coming regularly for a while, but he'd looked right past her.

She smiled. "I thought it was time to check out a neighborhood church rather than continuing to drive across the city."

"Good idea. I hope you enjoyed Pastor Tomas's sermon and the worship team."

"I did."

This time it was Denae who gave a little tug.

"I should let you go." Peter took a step back. "I'll see you around." He smiled and nodded at them both and headed to the foyer.

"Pietro!"

He gave his grandmother a quick hug and a pat on her back. "Hi, Nonna. How are you today?"

"Good, good. What's this I hear you asked a girl out?"

Peter winced. A megaphone couldn't have made her any louder. "Actually, she asked me but, either way, it's a date."

"A woman asks a man? What kind of world is this coming to?" Nonna's eyebrows rose along with both her hands. "Who is this bold one that you have not yet brought her to meet me?"

"It's not like that." He lowered his voice. Maybe she'd do the same. "We're going to a fundraiser for the Blessings Under the Bridge ministry. You know, the organization that feeds the homeless on Wednesday evenings. It's not like we're in a relationship."

"You don't even like her?"

"Nonna!" he hissed. "Shh. That's not what I said."

Nonna's gaze went past him and sharpened. "Someone I haven't met."

Peter closed his eyes and prayed for strength, pretty sure of what he'd see when he reopened them. Sure enough, there stood the woman in question, the pink on her face deeper than before. "Sadie."

Her eyebrows rose. So did her chin.

"Pietro. Has the cat got your tongue?"

Lord, strength, please? Asap. "Nonna, I'd like you to meet Sadie Guthrie. Sadie, this is my grandmother, Marietta Santoro. She was just... uh... asking about you."

"So I heard." Sadie's cool expression wafted over him as she turned to Nonna. "Pleased to meet you, Mrs. Santoro."

He held his breath as the two sized each other up.

Then Nonna smiled like the Cheshire cat. "So, you are the girl who's going to marry my Pietro. You may call me Marietta."

SADIE GASPED at the older woman in front of her. She looked so sweet and innocent with her pouf of gray curls, lightly tanned skin that spoke of genetics and years exposed to sunlight, and gentian-blue eyes that neither sparkled nor glared, but shrewdly assessed Sadie's response.

Denae stepped forward. "I'm Denae Archibald. You might have known my grandmother, Beulah Essery. I'm visiting my friend Sadie this weekend."

Thankfully, the old lady's gaze swerved to Denae, and air

returned to Sadie's lungs. "Which of Beulah's children is your parent?"

"Myrna."

Marietta nodded, taking in Denae. "You need to eat more, child."

No one had ever said that to Sadie.

"You will come for dinner to Dino and Betta's." Marietta's finger pointed back and forth between them. "She always makes plenty."

Peter took his grandmother's arm. "I'm sure they already have plans, Nonna."

Sadie darted him a glance. Poor guy looked uncomfortable with his flushed face and averted gaze. She felt the same.

"Nonsense. Everyone needs to eat." Marietta turned away. "Betta! These girls are coming for dinner."

"I'm sorry." Peter was so near his quiet words puffed warm air on Sadie's cheek. "She'll be eighty this year and thinks she can say whatever comes into her mind."

Stan was fifteen years younger and had done the same all Sadie's life. "It's okay. She caught me off guard is all."

He chuckled, still muffled. "Me, too. She means well." There was a slight hesitation. "Sometimes it's hard to tell."

How kind to try to put her at ease after his grandmother's wild — and loud — prediction.

"At any rate, my mom will go along with it, because no one says no to Nonna. And there *is* always enough to feed an army. I know you and Denae had plans, but you really are welcome."

"You'll be there?"

He shrugged slightly. "Around here, family gets together

after church, and Nonna rotates between her sons. Everyone's always so busy during the week that we put in an effort on Sundays."

Sadie looked at him and couldn't pull her gaze away. "How many relatives do you have, anyway?"

Peter scratched his ear. "Most of Nonna's five sons live within three blocks of her house. Except my uncle Al passed away last fall. The other brother lives in Galena Landing, Idaho. And there are — let me think — seventeen grandkids? A few have moved away, but probably a dozen of us are right here in Bridgeview."

"I can't even imagine."

"Come for lunch, and you'll get a glimpse." He grinned in his adorable, lopsided way.

Stop it, Sadie. They were neighbors who were trying to get along instead of threatening lawsuits like their first meeting. They weren't even friends, let alone more. She'd only invited him to the banquet out of a sense of preservation for her career. Not because she found him attractive.

Okay, fine, she found him attractive. But that didn't mean he felt the same. What man would? He was just being nice.

"We'd love to," came Denae's voice.

Sadie whirled back to find her friend in a small circle with Marietta and a middle-aged woman who jiggled a baby. Stretching his arms, the little guy lurched toward Peter.

His hands came past Sadie's shoulder to catch the baby. "Mom, I'd like you to meet Sadie Guthrie. Looks like you've already met her friend Denae. Sadie, this is my mom, Betta Santoro, and my cute little nephew, Gavin." He rubbed his short beard over the baby's cheek.

Gavin chortled with such a deep belly laugh that Sadie couldn't help smiling. He seemed adorable, not that she had anything to compare him with. She'd been an only child with no young relatives nearby. She'd spent her high school weekends on debate teams, not babysitting like some teens she knew.

"It's only a simple meal today." Betta shook her head. "You're welcome to share it, but it's not a grand spread."

"Pshaw," Marietta scolded. "Anything you cook is delicious, Betta. Unless you made that...?"

Peter's mother's face pinked. "That disaster was twenty-five years ago. Can we please forget it?"

A teen girl with long dark hair plucked Gavin out of Peter's arms. "Thanks, Petey. I've got him now."

"Daf, I'd like you to meet my next-door neighbor, Sadie, and her friend Denae. Ladies, my sister Dafne." He waited a beat. "Gavin's mom."

While Denae leaned in and gushed over the baby, Sadie remembered to snap her jaw shut. His sister was a teen mom raising her own child? Well, with help from the family, it looked like. But another thought pierced from nowhere nearly flattening her. Why hadn't her own birth mom made the same choice? Raised Sadie with the help of her own network? That whole *she loved you enough to give you up* had never rung true. What could be more vital to a kid than her own mother's love? Yeah, Lynda had tried. Sadie would give her that. But, looking back, it was obvious there'd never been a deep connection.

Sadie had seen it all come through the courtroom. And there had been plenty of adoptive parents completely enthralled with the baby or child entrusted to them. She'd seen couples return to adopt a second or even third child, still in love with parenting.

She'd had to realize that it wasn't adoption that was so wrong. It was something in Stan and Lynda that made them unable to love her. Or maybe... maybe that something was within Sadie herself. Maybe she was unlovable.

Had she ever been a giggling baby like little Gavin? Maybe she'd been the one who held back and made it difficult for Lynda and Stan. Sure, they were the grownups who'd gone to court and signed papers. They had to have wanted her, at least on some level. Maybe they'd have been better parents for a different child. A lovable one.

CHAPTER 9

I'm sorry it is only soup and rolls." Mom apologized again. She'd asked Peter to dump the slow cooker's contents into a decorative tureen.

He poured slowly as she scraped the sides, the steamy, aromatic soup making his stomach grumble in anticipation. "There's nothing *only* about this. Zuppa tuscana is one of my favorite meals, and you made the ciabatta rolls from scratch yesterday. Plus, I'm pretty sure there's biscotti back there somewhere."

Mom peered around him, probably checking Nonna's whereabouts. Then she sighed. "The biscotti is one of the few things I know *she* likes, every time."

Peter set the heavy slow cooker insert down and gave his mom a side hug. "Don't let her get to you. She loves you, and you know it." It must've been hard for Nonna to welcome daughters-in-law into her family, though, and steal her beloved sons away. Only Aunt Grace — Jasmine's mom — and Aunt Genevera had truly won their mother-in-law over. Nonna seemed a little more indulgent of her grand-children's spouses.

And she'd declared Sadie was the woman for him in front of half the congregation at church. Peter's friends, neighbors, relatives, and colleagues had borne witness.

Mom arranged a heap of rolls in a china basket. "Well, same to you. Even though she announced to the world that you should marry that girl, she still loves you. Right?"

Nonna had embarrassed the life out of him, but he'd seen the shock and dismay cross Sadie's face. She'd been quiet enough before, but she'd said barely a word since. Even now, Nonna and Denae carried the conversation in the other room, with Peter's other sister, Ava, joining in.

He sighed. "Yep. She loves me. I tell myself that all the time. To be honest, this is the first time she's ever humili-ated me in public. I'll get over it. I hope Sadie will."

Mom pulled the butter dishes from the cupboard. "Do you like Sadie a lot? I hadn't realized."

Peter stifled a groan. "I barely know her, Mom. I told you how upset I was about the house next door. Thanks for being willing to co-sign if she'd sell." The situation still grated. He might be over it before he turned forty. He might not. "Then she invited me to the fundraiser. It's a cause I believe in, and I couldn't justify the price of a ticket. It seemed silly to turn her down just because she bought Mrs. Essery's house. There's nothing between us."

"I notice you keep watching her."

"Hoping no one embarrasses her even more than Nonna already has. Wondering how she'll take this crazy family. Don't worry about it, Mom. When I meet the perfect woman for me, you'll be among the first to know."

Mom touched the side of his face, her gaze intent on his. "Thank you. Now be a good boy and carry out the tureen, will you? And call everyone to the table. I'll go find Dafne. She said she needed to change Gavin, but she's been gone for quite a while."

A MAN who helped his mother in the kitchen. Be still, her heart. Sadie watched Peter set a white baroque tureen in the center of a dining table with pure white china settings laid around the perimeter of a lace tablecloth.

"Please, have a seat." His gaze arrowed straight for hers. "Sadie, you and Denae may sit here on the end."

He went back into the kitchen and returned a moment later with a woven porcelain basket heaped with rolls, just as his mom, the teen, and the baby came in from the other entrance. The girl tucked the little guy in a high chair a few chairs away from the one Sadie now found herself behind. Gavin pounded a spoon to his tray, chortling with enthusiasm and not a little drool.

Good thing the child's mother and Denae separated Sadie from the mess the baby was sure to make. Also, thankfully, Peter's dad seated his outspoken grandmother at the other end. Whew.

Sadie reached to pull out her chair, but Peter's hand was there first. She looked up in surprise. Men didn't still do that, did they? Not in the office, where women had fought to be treated as equals and were, mostly.

His eyes warmed, but he said nothing as he seated her then took the chair next to hers.

"Shall we say grace?" invited Peter's dad. What was his name again? Dino. That was it. Then he launched into a heartfelt prayer of thanksgiving that included their guests and the baby.

Really? The man was thankful for a child born to his teenager? Wouldn't most encourage their daughter to abort, kick her out of the house, or gloss things over with an adoption? Sadie had seen her share of all those angles from her office, but this... this wasn't a scenario that came down the marble hallway at Dawson and Banks.

What kind of man had her birth grandfather been? Certainly not anything like Dino Santoro, or Sadie's life would have been vastly different. She swiped a tear from her eye at the amen and nodded when Peter offered to fill her soup bowl.

﹏

GAVIN'S WAILS quieted as Dafne carried him down the stairs for his nap. The front door closed behind Sadie, Denae, and Nonna. Peter sagged back against the leather sofa in his parents' living room and closed his eyes.

"Why didn't you tell me?" Ava plopped beside him. "I'm always the last to know the gossip."

He groaned. "There's nothing to tell. Nonna has the best imagination on the planet."

Ava tossed a pillow at his chest, and he caught it reflexively. "I've seen Sadie in Bridgeview Bakery and Bistro a few times, but I had no idea she was the woman who'd bought the Essery house." She leaned closer. "Or that you were going out with her."

"For the sixty-seventh time, we're attending a fundraiser. It's a long way from a real date." Besides, dates were when guys asked girls out. Not when the girl did the asking.

"You haven't dated since Penelope that I know of. What's it been, five years since you guys broke up? This is huge."

"For the sixty-*eighth* time..."

"You like her."

"You've been taking lessons from Nonna."

"We do share genetics. She seems pretty nice, even though she's reserved. Sadie, I mean, not Nonna."

Peter couldn't help laughing. The day anyone thought his grandmother was reserved was the day she was in a coma. "Sadie's not always this quiet. Not sure what was up today. Probably she was as embarrassed as I was at Nonna's announcement at church. She was likely trying to avoid being noticed after that."

"Maybe." His younger sister eyed him. "How do you know she's not always this quiet?"

"She lives next door. We've talked a few times." Not many, but he'd caught himself timing his excursions to when she usually arrived home from the office. Once this infernal rain let up, he'd be so busy after work that there'd be no time for accidental hellos. Except when he was harvesting asparagus or radishes from her yard.

The one that was supposed to be his.

Dad came in and settled into his favorite chair. "Raimondo tells me the hot water tank at your place quit this morning?"

Uncle Ray was Jasmine and Alex's dad. "Yes. Leaked all over the basement. Thankfully Logan and Linnea hadn't unpacked their car yet, so it's mostly an inconvenience. Alex turned off the water to it, and we sopped up the mess, but it will be a day or two before he can get a plumber in to replace it."

Ava jabbed his ribs. "Sounds like you should move back home until you've got hot water."

He nodded, looking at his dad. "I was thinking that. Okay with you and Mom?"

"Of course. You'll need to take Dafne's old room since she and Gavin moved into your basement space, but there's no reason why not. I'm sure your mother will like having all her chicks in the nest for a few days."

"Chickie." Ava poked him again.

Peter flicked the pillow at his sister but kept his focus on his father. "Thanks. It might even be for only one night. I hate to bail out on Alex, but there's not much I can do to help. I don't have the skills, and I've got too much on my plate as it is."

"I think you should go out with Denae instead of Sadie."

"What brought that on?" Peter scowled at Ava. "I'm not marrying either one of them."

She waggled a finger. "Famous last words, bro. Denae is tough enough to stand up to Nonna. She was giving as good as she got."

"She doesn't live here and, even if she did, she really doesn't interest me." Like, at all. Way too skinny for his taste, for one thing. Too... weird, for another.

"When Sadie comes into the bakery, it's all I can do to keep Astrid from jumping on her." Ava's nose wrinkled. "Astrid's all about people eating less stuff with sugar. I'm not sure why Hailey and Kass keep her around. I mean, it's a bakery. Nearly everything has sugar."

"Because good help is hard to find?" Peter had met Astrid, a middle-aged woman with about as much control over her tongue as Nonna. While Nonna was pleasantly plump, Astrid was short and thin. Get the two of them in the same room and a guy needed to call in a referee. "Making things difficult for a customer is none of Astrid's business."

"That's what Kass told her. It's like muzzling a Chihuahua. You can still tell when it's dying to yip."

If Peter had to class Sadie somewhere, yeah, she wore more pounds than she needed to. The bigger problem seemed to be how winded she'd become walking up that one block the other night. He led such an active life, playing basketball, hiking constantly on the day job with Fish and Wildlife and now gardening, he tended not to notice the angle of Bridgeview streets.

He hated that Astrid would actively belittle Sadie. That was a form of discrimination, and simply not okay. "If Astrid crosses the line, let me know. I'll set her straight."

Ava giggled. "You *do* have the hots for Sadie. I knew it."

"Ava Elizabeth, we don't talk like that in this house," Dad said sternly.

"Aw, Dad, I don't know how else to describe it when Peter says he'll protect Sadie at a random place of business. While pretending he doesn't care."

Peter surged to his feet. "Don't you have some studying to do or something like that?"

"You really aren't paying attention. College exams are

over, and summer vacation is upon us. Hence Linnea and Logan are back in town."

Oh. Right.

"I'm at the bakery full time until September when I go back for senior year."

How had his little sister gotten so old? He wouldn't call it mature, not after that comment about the hots. "I'm going up to the house to grab some stuff for tomorrow, but I won't be back until evening. Got some things to do."

"Peter and Sadie, sitting in a tree—"

He silenced his sister with a glare. "Get a life. Just wait until you have a boyfriend, and I get to tell him how juvenile you are."

Ava gathered her hair together and flipped it over her shoulder then batted her eyelashes at him. "That's why you won't meet him until I'm wearing a ring."

If that was supposed to pique his curiosity, it wasn't going to work. "I have my ways." Peter stopped in the kitchen, but the dishwasher was humming and his mom nowhere in sight. He'd catch her later.

He let himself out the back door into the late April drizzle. It was only a few blocks up to the house, and he wasn't going to dissolve like sugar in water before he got there. Which reminded him of Astrid's campaign. Yeah, okay, he could see most people probably ate too much sugar. He wasn't immune to those amazing cinnamon rolls from the bakery himself, but it wasn't Astrid's job to sabotage the business where she worked.

Yeah, Sadie was overweight compared to most other women he knew, but what did it matter? She was intelligent. She was self-sufficient. She cared about the less fortunate.

Weren't those things far more important than the numbers on a scale?

Also, she was pretty. Blond curls to her shoulders, sparkling blue eyes, a great smile. She'd be interesting to talk to at the fundraiser *and* look great by his side. Also, he needed to get his tux dry-cleaned.

A wrist corsage that matched a purple gown? He'd be working out of town all week with the controlled burns near the Idaho border. Surely flowers could be ordered online. He'd take a few minutes to get that taken care of as soon as he got back to Alex's.

CHAPTER 10

The doorbell rang in the middle of Saturday afternoon. Who could it be? With Denae out of town and Stan not yet back in Spokane, it wasn't like the world beat a path to her door. Sadie frowned as she made her way through the living room, nearly tripping over Anastasia. She scooped the cat up as she opened the door. She really needed to get a peephole installed.

A giant bouquet of flowers met her gaze. Several white lilies shone amid purple lisianthus, mums, and other flowers. She'd never seen — or inhaled — anything so gorgeous, but it couldn't be hers. "I'm sorry, you must have the wrong address."

The man behind the bouquet glanced at the device in his hand then back at the brass house number on the stucco beside her. "Are you Sadie Guthrie?"

She nodded, not daring to breathe and unable to wrench her gaze from the flowers emitting such divine fragrance.

"Then these are for you. And there's this, as well." He passed her a small box with a clear plastic lid. Inside it lay a wrist corsage of purple and white hyacinths with lovely ribbon accents.

Tonight was the fundraiser. Denae had told Peter exactly what to get Sadie for a corsage, and he'd obeyed. But the lilies...

The deliveryman pushed the bouquet toward her. "Ma'am?"

Anastasia leaped for the floor.

"Yes, of course. Thank you." Hands shaking, she set the corsage on a side table behind her and reached for the glass vase anchoring the large arrangement.

The florist van pulled away as she set the bouquet in the center of her dining room table with the afternoon sunlight — a rare sight these days — backlighting the arrangement. She snapped a quick photo with her phone and sent it to Denae then went back for the corsage.

Her phone rang. She grinned at Denae's number. "Hey." Then she held the device at arm's length while her friend squealed.

"He didn't!" Denae shrieked. "That man is a keeper, Sadie. Don't you dare let him get away."

"How do you know who sent them? I might have any number of secret admirers. It might even have been Stan."

"No way. It was Peter. Right? Tell me it was Peter."

Sadie tugged the little envelope from the midst of the bouquet. The touch seemed to signal the flowers to release their fragrance. She took a deep sniff and pulled out the card.

"What does it say? Don't leave me in suspense."

"It says..." Sadie drew out the words, like reading the

card out loud would make it cackle and go poof. "It says, 'these made me think of you. See you at 6:00.'"

"Wow." Denae heaved a melodramatic sigh. "That is the single most romantic thing I've ever heard."

"I doubt it. You edit romance novels."

"But in real life. Authors can make men say anything they want, and some of those heroes, quite frankly, sound too good to be true. They're so sensitive and perfect you can tell some needy woman made them up."

Sadie read romance herself. She knew what Denae meant.

"But this is totally swoon-worthy. I repeat, do *not* let this man get away. It's your job to get a kiss out of him tonight. I expect a wedding by Christmas, and you have permission to name your first child after me."

Sadie couldn't help giggling. "You're absurd. There's no way he'll kiss me. We barely know each other, and this isn't that kind of date, anyway." Was it? Her gaze lingered on the flowers. Maybe it was.

"So, you kiss him. He'll kiss you back, promise."

"No way. I'm not that brazen."

"You asked him out."

"Denae, it's a fundraiser, and I needed a plus-one. Remember? This isn't about romance."

"Put me on Skype, look me in the eye, and tell me those flowers are not romantic. That those words aren't. Come on. Dare ya."

Sadie hesitated. "They're gorgeous."

"Umhmmm." Denae sounded mighty smug. "Have you redeemed the gift certificate for the mani-pedi yet?"

"This morning. Silver glitter polish."

"You're all set. Here's a list of photos I want, okay? Your nails. The wrist corsage on your hand. A full-length selfie in the mirror with that great dress. Your plate of food. And one more."

"I'm afraid to ask."

"A selfie with Mr. Romantic."

"No way. That's much too forward."

"May I remind you you're the one who asked him out? Now read the card again. You ask this guy for a selfie, he'll oblige. Trust me."

"Maybe. I'll see how it goes. Now there's a bubble bath with my name on it."

"Man, I loved my grandma's clawfoot tub. Don't get rid of it when you remodel, okay?"

"I love it, too. Talk to you later."

"Call me tonight. I don't care what time you get in and, yes, I remember that it's an hour later in Montana. I want to hear all about that kiss."

"There won't be one."

"Remember we've talked about the power of positive thinking. Don't speak a death sentence over this evening before it's even begun. Look at those flowers, and don't give up hope."

Sadie clicked the phone off and walked toward the staircase. She hesitated and turned back to the dining room. Flowers didn't last forever. Wouldn't they be lonely downstairs if she was spending the next two hours bathing and primping? She couldn't do that to them. They could sit on the dresser in her bedroom. If she left the door ajar, she could see them from the tub.

Her finger slid over the words on the little card. Peter saw gorgeous flowers and thought of her? Probably only because he was in there anyway getting the corsage, so she was already on his mind. The bouquet was definitely above and beyond. She'd never received anything like them before. Not even supermarket flowers unless she bought them herself.

Did he really see her as beautiful?

She clutched the vase and carefully carried it up the stairs.

PETER FELT like he accompanied the most beautiful woman in the room. He'd only seen her in a power suit or sweats before — other than at church last week — but, wow, when she went all out, she was stunning.

Her face glowed, her curls spiraled, and her gown was gorgeous on her. The lace inset kept it modest compared to the plunging necklines some other women around the room wore. He couldn't keep his eyes off the woman at his side, couldn't help noticing the warmth every time she tucked her hand into the crook of his elbow.

She introduced him to the partners at the law office as her friend and neighbor. Cordell Dawson gave a speculative glance between them but didn't ask awkward questions. Because, right now, if anyone asked Peter what his intentions were, he'd be hard pressed to pretend there was no attraction.

Which was crazy. He'd joked about dating her, even about marrying her, to get his hands on that house and yard, but his feelings at the moment weren't a laughing matter. He could actually see—

Peter, no. Don't even go there. He rested his hand on the small of her back and guided her toward the round table they'd been assigned. She felt warm to the touch. Pleasant, even.

Sadie didn't shift away but glanced over her shoulder at him, her dark eyes shining, her lips parted with a smile.

He couldn't resist sliding his arm around her as her vanilla scent wafted toward him.

Her eyes widened.

Peter tightened his grip and leaned closer, his lips brushing her ear. Wished it were her lips instead, to his surprise. "You look amazing."

"Don't," she whispered.

"But you do." He steered her to the table and pulled out her chair. His arm felt chilled where he'd held her for that brief moment, and it seemed natural to keep it across the back of her chair, lightly touching her back.

Sadie leaned over. "You don't need to pretend," she whispered.

"Who's pretending?" he whispered back, his hand caressing her bare shoulder, his eyes focused on hers. "Did you like the flowers?" She'd greeted him at the door with thanks, but he wanted to hear it again. Maybe hear more than she'd said before.

"They're very pretty, and they smell amazing. But you didn't have to..."

Peter pressed his finger against her lips. "I didn't get them out of obligation." He couldn't help teasing a little. "Now, the wrist corsage — I'll admit Denae gave me a boot in the rear for that one. It's been a long time since I attended anything this formal. I doubt my sisters would have let me forget the corsage, though."

He removed his finger, but her gaze stayed riveted to it as he pulled away.

She was no less affected than he was.

The realization made his heart stutter. Was this the start of something big? Something real? How could he possibly know if he should pursue this woman? If his motives were right? Maybe... because when he looked in her eyes, he could totally forget she lived in the house he wanted.

WHEN THE BAND struck up and Peter rose and held his hand out to her, Sadie thought her heart would burst. She rested her hand on his shoulder and felt his touch on her back while their other hands clasped. She'd need to remember to thank Stan for insisting she take ballroom dance as her lone high school P.E. elective, even though she'd hated every minute.

Dancing with a handsome man who focused intently on her — a man who'd obviously taken lessons himself — was a far cry from her first experience with the scrawny, pimply boy she'd been partnered with back then.

Peter Santoro.

Of all the men she could have asked... well, no. There hadn't been any other options short of going up and down the street knocking on doors. She'd have come alone and slipped out after the meal, so no one would have noticed and felt sorry for her. Reality was a million times better.

The meal had been amazing, most likely. If Sadie hadn't remembered to take the photo Denae wanted, she'd likely have forgotten what was on her plate in ten minutes, but she was truly trying to stay in the moment. To tuck every single memory into a special corner of her brain so she'd be able to take them out later and savor them.

One perfect evening. A princess with a charming prince.

What would happen when the clock struck midnight? Would her fairy tale vanish like Cinderella's had?

"What are you thinking?" asked Peter.

Sadie didn't dare tell him, but she didn't want to lie, either. She smiled up at him.

"Having fun?"

"I am." She fingered the collar of his tux next to the silver silk tie he must have picked to match the ribbons on her corsage. "I hope you are, too."

He leaned closer. "I'm glad you invited me."

Her gaze flicked to meet his. "I'm never going to live that down, am I?"

Peter swung her around with the music. "Why would you want to?"

"I'm not always that forward."

His hand on her back pulled her a little closer. "I don't mind."

That's when she noticed he'd steered her right off the dance floor and partially behind a large potted plant. Now both his hands rested on her hips. She wouldn't think about how large they were, not right now. Not with his blue eyes inches from hers.

"There are some things I've never done before, either, but that doesn't mean doing them is a bad idea."

"Like what?" Her words stuttered out.

"I've never kissed on a first date." His breath warmed her face. "May I?"

She slid her hands around his neck, reveling in his nearness. "You may," she whispered, tilting her mouth toward his and closing her eyes.

His lips covered hers, soft and gentle, sweet and persuasive.

Could she be falling in love? She'd only known him for a month, but she was certainly falling in something. Something that made her think the universe was the limit, that a rainbow was made of a thousand colors, that all the world held the sweet honey aroma of hyacinths.

Peter feathered a series of kisses along the side of her lips then pulled her head against his chest. "Thank you," he whispered.

He tilted her world on its axis and thanked *her*? *Be still my heart.*

And even though Denae had been right — again — this was a moment Sadie would cherish forever, and no selfie would help her remember it with any greater clarity. If Denae wanted pix of starry eyes and lips that had just been kissed, she'd need to find her own prince charming.

Sadie was keeping all this to herself. Forever.

CHAPTER 11

"You do this every week?"

Peter glanced over at Sadie as she arranged bunches of radishes in flat wicker baskets. "Bridgeview Backyards is a permanent installation at the Kendall Yards Night Market, yes. Me, personally? Not usually. Schmoozing the public was Basil's thing." He hoisted a basket of bok choy to the table.

"You haven't told me much about your cousin. Jasmine's brother, right?"

He nodded. "She's the middle child with four brothers. You've met Marco. Basil's next, then Jasmine, then Alex, then Evan. Basil was Jasmine's and my partner, but he's also the wild one. Got a DUI charge last summer, spent a bit of time in jail, then headed off to Seattle. Jasmine and I had to buy him out."

"I can't get over the size of your family."

"That's Jasmine's. I only have two sisters." Whom Sadie had met a couple of times now, since Mom had invited her for Sunday dinner every week. He arranged a basket of leaf lettuce then another of radishes.

"You're really going to sell all this?" Sadie indicated the table of vegetables taking shape. "When I've come to the market, it's generally been for the other stuff, like candles and handmade soaps. The awesome pizza. The vibe."

"Most of it, I think." Peter had noticed she didn't cook at home at all... and picked at her vegetables when they ate out. "People are hungry for fresh greens after a long winter."

Sadie buried her hands in the pockets of her knee-length navy shorts as she angled her head and took in the display. "I don't get it, myself, but I respect how hard you've worked to put this all together." Then she shook her head. "Mind if I walk the market, now that it's ready to open? Want anything? I could bring you back a coffee and cheesecake."

"No, thanks." He pointed at his backpack. "I have everything I need. Water, a sandwich, snacks. But, go ahead."

She stretched for a kiss before she wandered off, barely glancing at the farm-fresh vendors and heading for the artisans.

Peter watched her until she disappeared into the gathering crowd. They hadn't spent a lot of time together over the past two weeks since the amazing gala, which had raised thousands of dollars for the homeless ministry. He'd connected with the coordinator a few days later and arranged drop-offs of unsold vegetables. Too bad their big meal of the week was the same evening as the Night Market. He and Jasmine had talked about how much donating they could do and stay in business.

But, Sadie. She was a conundrum. A lovely distraction he was quickly falling for until times like this when he remembered she might as well be from a different planet... and it wasn't the old *men are from Mars, women from Venus* line. It was considerably more fundamental than even genders.

She didn't care about vegetables. About nutrition. They'd gone to Costco together — ultimate date night, right? — and she'd stocked up on sugar-loaded coffee pods for her single-serve machine while confessing how many she drank daily. Her other major purchase had been snacks. He'd been there for produce and meat, but then he and Alex actually cooked meals at home and cared how they fueled their bodies.

How could he fall in love with a woman who refused to eat her veggies? What if they married and had kids? For that matter, who would cook? Peter didn't mind cooking, but he'd never imagined a scenario where he'd not only work eight-to-twelve-hour days but come home and prepare every meal for his family. Yeah, yeah. Call him old-fashioned. His mom did nearly all the cooking during the week, and Dad kicked in for weekend breakfasts. It worked for them. Peter had always envisioned a shared kitchen, not one where he was primary. He shook the thoughts away as the first customer rushed over.

"You've got fresh radishes! Oh, man, I can't believe how eagerly I've been waiting for them. And asparagus. Have you ever roasted them together? That is my new absolutely favorite thing."

Peter grinned at the thirty-something woman. "I haven't had them that way, but it sounds great. I had cooked radishes for the first time a couple of months ago. The changed flavor sure surprised me."

"I know! Aren't they amazing? You never know what will happen when you stick something in hot water, right? Radishes turn from these hard, bitter balls into something sweet and succulent."

Peter chuckled. "If you're willing to share your recipe, I'd love to try it. I'm always looking for a new dish."

She beamed at him. "You cook? Your wife is one lucky woman."

"I'm not married. I bunk with my cousin, and we share meal prep."

"Well, that's cool, too." The woman reached for a sprig of herbs. "Mmm, early dill. I want some of this... some of that..." She gathered her purchases together and Peter tallied them up. "Oh, if you give me your email address, I'll send you the recipe."

Peter handed her a business card. "Please do. My email's on here."

"Perfect." She tucked the vegetables into a large cloth bag. "Thanks so much, and I'll see you next week?"

"I'll be here. We're also at the market downtown Saturday morning."

"Oh, good. I'll keep that in mind." She waved as she walked away.

He hadn't caught her name, not that it mattered. Only, why wasn't she the kind of woman he was falling for instead of Sadie, the veggie hater?

⁂

"CAN I MAKE YOU A COFFEE?" Sadie asked the representative for Ranta Landscaping. "I've got several flavors on hand. Just made myself a caramel espresso."

Linnea shook her head, smiling. "Herbal tea if you have some."

"Um, sorry. I don't."

"Then water will be fine."

Sadie pulled a bottle out of the fridge and pointed to the small back porch. "Let's sit out there, so you can see the space while we talk."

"Sounds good." Linnea followed her, set her notebook on the tiny wrought iron table, and took one of the matching chairs. "Are you looking for more garden space?"

Sadie frowned, staring at the neat rows of asparagus spears sticking out of the brown soil. Peter's pride and joy. She took a deep breath. "No, not at all. I'm an attorney practicing family law. It's an emotionally draining career, and what I really need back here is a private oasis. A place to recharge."

"I see." Linnea flipped her pen. "Tell me more."

"I want fragrance. Roses." Sadie remembered the glorious aroma of the bouquet Peter had sent her. "Lilies. I'm not sure what all, but a variety of flowers that will bloom from spring to fall and smell sweet. Attracting birds and butterflies would be nice. I want a water feature, maybe a fountain or a waterfall, whatever you think works. I want a lot of hard surface for a patio, with some sort of shade structure." Just in case she ever made friends and got around to entertaining. "Basically, a relaxing place that appeals to the five senses."

"And right now, the yard is leased to Bridgeview Backyards?"

"Not leased, exactly. The former owner had an arrangement with them, but I've let Peter know it will end when your company is ready to start work. Dan — that's your brother, right? — told me it wasn't likely until midsummer."

"Yes, we're pretty tied up for the next couple of months. I'm not sure, though. I heard you and Peter were dating."

Sadie smiled. "We are. He's a really great guy."

"But you're still planning to kick him out of your yard?"

"Well, it *is* my space."

"This may be too personal, but I have to ask. What if you guys get married? Wouldn't he expect to have a say in how the space is utilized?"

"If he really loved me, wouldn't he want me to be happy? I'm sure he would, so I'm not worried about it. There are other backyards in the city owned by people who want vegetables." Hard to imagine, but there it was. Peter had sold every scrap of his produce this morning at the downtown market, so obviously someone liked it.

"I'm happy to offer you a design," Linnea said slowly. "But I hope it's something you and Peter talk about and agree on before we go ahead. I don't want to be responsible for putting a barrier between you."

A burst of anger flared through Sadie as she surged to her feet. "I can hire someone else, in that case. I own this property, and I want a relaxing outdoor space. If you can't — or won't — make it happen, there are other landscaping companies in Spokane."

"I'm sorry. I didn't mean to offend you."

Sadie sank slowly back to her seat, her heart still pounding from the exertion. "I'm sorry for overreacting." Still, why didn't people treat her like a grownup? She was a homeowner. A lawyer, not some college kid.

"It happens I'm very partial to butterfly habitat. We created a flower garden similar to what you're looking for two years ago at the community garden. I'd love to know what you think of the choices there."

"Community garden?"

"Yes, you can't miss it. Surrounded by a white picket fence? It's a couple of blocks down the hill, next door to Marietta Santoro's house."

Sadie frowned, trying to remember. "I've driven by it, I think."

"Well, have a closer look. It's a full-size city lot with sixteen raised garden beds for community members, but there are also shared spaces with herbs, flowers, a fountain, a gazebo." Linnea's face brightened. "You know what else likes similar blossoms? Bees. We set aside a corner of the community garden for two beehives. You might enjoy something like that as well."

Where did this landscape designer come from? "Um, no? Bees sting. I think I mentioned a *peaceful* oasis, not one where I'm hiding from venomous insects."

"Honeybees rarely sting, unless you're seen as a danger by coming too close to the hives or by grabbing a flower they're sitting on."

"No. Just no."

"Okay. It was only an idea. Have a look at the community garden and let me know what you think. I'll send you a list of the flowers we used there and why when I give you a preliminary sketch." Linnea stood and pulled a big round tape measure from her purse. "May I take some measurements?"

"Sure, go ahead." The more Sadie thought about it, the more she doubted Ranta Landscaping was the right company for the job. Linnea seemed to have her own agenda — an attitude Sadie had run into a lot in Bridgeview since she'd moved in six weeks ago. She'd debated avoiding the local bakery and bistro until she'd figured out what hours the scowling middle-aged woman who mumbled about the evils of sugar worked. At least Peter's sister, who also worked there, didn't seem to condemn her choices. Sadie couldn't help they made the best cinnamon rolls she'd ever tasted, and their lemon squares were divine. Plus, a serving of fruit, right? Win, win.

When Linnea finally hopped in the Ranta Landscaping truck and drove away, Sadie snagged a slice of leftover pizza from the fridge and took it into the living room with another cup of coffee. She'd just settled on the sofa, Anastasia on her lap, when the doorbell rang.

She glared toward it for a moment before heaving upright. The Siamese grumbled at her and stalked off. Man, she was so tired these days. It was probably all the stress at work, plus the new relationship with Peter. Was it too much to ask for random people to leave her alone on her day off? At least her boyfriend would tap on the back door before breezing in, calling her name.

Sadie opened the door and found Stan on the stoop. Of course, his gaze went straight to the pizza in her hand, his eyebrows shooting up.

"Hi, Stan. What brings you by?"

He winced. "Is that any welcome for your dad? I bought a house over in Manito, remember? I thought I'd come over and spend a little time with my daughter."

Adoptive daughter, but Sadie wouldn't rub his face in it. She sighed, hopefully unnoticeably. "Sure, come in. Want pizza? There are several more pieces in the box."

"No, thank you. I had lunch a couple of hours ago. I'd love some water, though."

So had she. Whatever. She grabbed a bottle from the fridge then settled on the corner of the sofa and tucked her legs under her. Anastasia sat glaring at her from the archway to the dining room, blinking slowly before lifting a paw to lick it. Likely didn't trust her to stay put.

Sadie looked over at Stan as he sat on an antique armchair. "Are you getting settled in okay?"

"I wish you'd come by and see the house. Maybe tomorrow?"

"Maybe Peter can bring me by after we have lunch with his family after church."

"That would be nice. I haven't met him yet." Stan cracked a smile. "I need to check out if this guy is good enough to date my little girl."

Sadie managed to stop the eye-roll before it happened. Managed to bite back the reminder of her adoption. See? She was a grownup. She could control herself. "I had a landscaper come by a bit ago to discuss my plans for the backyard."

Stan's eyebrows rose.

Not him, too. "I told you, I want a place to relax in the warmer months. Come fall, I'll hire someone to work on the interior. Brighten it up a little." The atmosphere oozed old-lady charm and antiquated color schemes. New paint colors, new window coverings, a judicious selection of contemporary furnishings, and she'd have the house of her dreams: modern with great bones and woodwork.

He nodded and leaned forward. "I'm glad you have a boyfriend, honey. You've been working too hard, keeping too much to yourself." He studied her face. "Are you sleeping well? You look really tired."

"I've felt better," she admitted. "There's a lot going on at work, including a nasty custody fight where both parents are pulling out all the stops and using their kids as pawns. It's been ugly."

"I'm sorry to hear that. Kids need stability."

"Why did you and Lynda adopt me?"

Oh, no. Had she said that out loud? By the way Stan's face instantly closed off, yes, she had.

"You needed a home, and we'd been unable to conceive."

That was an odd way to word it. She angled her head. "What do you know about my biological parents?"

Stan shook his head. "Those records are all sealed up."

She wasn't in family law for nothing, but she'd been unable to find her original birth certificate. The one stating Stanley and Lynda Guthrie as her parents had been filed only two weeks after her birth. Which meant there had to be another one out there, right? "Stan, it's really important to me."

"You're our child, Sadie. We raised you from the day you were born. Loved you. Gave you everything you needed. I don't know why Lynda dumped that burden on you before she died. You never needed to know."

"I can't believe you said that." She straightened. "Why

would a person not have the right to know her own family history? Medical, for instance?"

"Your medical history is fine, Sadie. Stop worrying about it."

"You knew my biological parents?" Of course. That answered many of her questions... but not all of them.

He rose from his chair, looking every minute of his sixty-five years. "Sadie..."

"Don't bother with evasion. This happened twenty-seven years ago. I'm an adult, and I deserve to know. Both Washington and Oregon have opened up access." She'd been so sure she could simply apply for her files and then pick them up, but the court clerk reminded her that some states still had closed records. Like Illinois, where she'd been born. Could a birth certificate lie about more than parentage?

"Then you've been unable to find anything?" His gaze narrowed in on hers.

She stood and stepped right into his space. "Not a thing."

Why would he look so relieved? Could she be the result of a fling during Stan's mid-life crisis? The idea grew as he averted his gaze, made his excuses, and headed out the door.

Sadie's gaze zeroed in on the water bottle he'd left behind. Was there enough DNA on that to send away? Worth a try.

CHAPTER 12

*P*eter came in the house to discover Linnea working at her drafting table near the front window. She'd asked to work upstairs, citing better light. He and Alex certainly didn't use every inch of the living room, and it hadn't been a hassle to rearrange Alex's sparse furniture to make room. Besides, she and Logan spent a lot of time upstairs, anyway.

"What are you working on?" he asked from the kitchen. "Want coffee or tea?"

She glanced up. "Maybe herbal tea with a dollop of honey, if you've got it."

He chuckled. "Jasmine is my cousin and Alex's sister. We have no fewer than six kinds of personally harvested herbal tea, and you can pick your honey flavor, too."

"I should have known." Linnea laughed. "Chamomile then. Thanks." She turned back to her drafting table, tapping her pencil.

A few minutes later, he carried two mugs across the room. Herbal tea was a better idea for him in the evening, too. Man, his muscles ached from weeding over at the Johnsons'. He glanced at the design as he set Linnea's tea on a side table. "Is that for Ranta Landscaping?"

"Thanks, Peter." She swiveled her chair and lifted the mug. "Yes, but something you might care about more than most."

He raised his eyebrows as he settled into an easy chair. "Oh?"

"Sadie is looking for a backyard redesign."

Even though he'd known that all along, the knowledge punched him in the gut. Why had he thought she'd reconsider? He took in a deep breath and let it out slowly. "I see. Back to ripping out barely established asparagus beds and paving over every inch that doesn't have a rosebush in it."

"Fairly accurate."

Peter rubbed his forehead. "Oh, man. What do I do?"

Linnea raised her eyebrows. "What do you mean?"

"Well, I don't have any legal rights, but I was hoping she'd reconsider." Or forget. That would have been a fine option as well.

"Don't tell me you're dating her because you want her yard."

"No. I mean, the thought crossed my mind, but it's really not the case. I like her a lot. Except..."

"Except?"

"She's a confusing blend of confident and needy. Also, she hates vegetables."

"Yeah, I got that impression. Peter, it's probably none of my business, but... I'm not sure she's the right person for you."

"I'm not sure, either." He rubbed his head again. "I

think she'd take it really hard if we broke up. She'd probably think it was because of the backyard. Or because she's heavier than some women. She seems... fragile."

"It's not your job to hold someone else up, Peter. She's an adult."

"But isn't that what love does? Not saying I love her. It's too early to know that, but still. My parents support each other through the ups and downs. I've seen that with Wade and Rebekah. With you and Logan. Others."

She bit her lip, nodding. "Do you remember when Logan and I broke up? Logan thought I was too needy, and he was right. I had to do some growing up before we could come together more evenly matched. I'm still overly sensitive, so I get where Sadie is coming from there. And she wants what she wants."

"I don't know what to do about this. I met her dad a few days ago. She calls him by his first name."

Linnea met his gaze.

"She says she's adopted, so it's okay to call him Stan. Whatever happened in their shared history, they're not very close, and her mom passed away when she was in high school. No close relatives."

"Sounds crazy after the Santoro clan."

"Yeah, it does. I feel sorry for her."

"Peter? Dating someone because you feel sorry for her isn't healthy. It's just not."

Was that all it was? No. When he was with Sadie, the sun seemed to shine brighter, but the clouds also seemed to move in more suddenly. He enjoyed making her smile, giving her things, holding her hand. Kissing her. She was unlike anyone he'd ever dreamed of dating, but that didn't mean she wasn't amazing. She was. "I appreciate your concern."

"We'll pray for you. I well remember how rocky and emotional and... weird... everything seems while you're working through the early stages of a relationship. All I ask is that you're asking for God's wisdom... and then following what He shows you. Trust me, I'd be happy to be wrong."

The backdoor whipped open and Logan jogged into the room. "He did it! Linnea, love, he did it!"

By the blank look on Linnea's face, she had no more idea what her husband was talking about than Peter did. "Who did what?"

"Your brother! I just prayed with Dan for salvation. Sounds like he's been hoarding his questions since before Al Santoro's funeral." Logan nodded at Peter, suddenly serious. "Your uncle's life and testimony had a major impact, man. His celebration of life was a critical part of Wesley Ferguson's faith journey, and definitely Dan's. I've heard of several other stories, too."

Peter swallowed the lump in his throat as he nodded. "My uncle wasn't perfect, but he was eager to be used by God while he was alive. He'd be delighted to know about Dan. I know I am." He'd have to remember to tell Aunt Winnie. Al's widow had been so strong through the last eight months.

"What did Dixie say?" Worry warred with happiness on Linnea's face.

Dan had been living with Dixie for several years and was the father of her youngest child, one-year-old Henry.

"He was going home to tell her. He knows she might be unhappy."

That was an understatement. Dixie was known for loose morals, even going out with Peter's stupid cousin not long after her baby's birth — the night of Basil's drunk driving arrest. She wasn't committed enough to Dan to take his news in stride.

Peter exhaled, long and slow. "We need to pray for Dan and Dixie both. There's a very real possibility this situation won't end well."

Logan swung to face him. "The angels in heaven are rejoicing that one who was lost has been found. How can we do otherwise?"

"I'm rejoicing, man. I really am. But this is going to get messy."

Linnea nodded. "I think Peter's right. We definitely need to pray, starting right now."

The three of them bowed their heads and lifted the new believer up in prayer.

SADIE STARED at the results of the DNA test. There was no probability that she was related to Stanley Guthrie. He was not her biological father. Not her uncle or cousin or anything else. No genetics in common.

Which made sense from everything he'd said. Was it Lynda who'd been sleeping around, and Stan had adopted the result? That didn't add up. He wouldn't have needed to adopt her — they'd been married for over fifteen years at Sadie's birth. Besides, Lynda's confession would have been different. No, Lynda wasn't her parent any more than Stan was.

Could they have stolen a newborn? Lynda had been a nurse. Maybe she'd had the opportunity and run with it. Literally. That would explain their move from Illinois to Oregon back then. But that didn't seem in line with Lynda's character.

Sadie set the results down on the counter and stuck a caramel espresso pod into the coffee maker. She needed caffeine to cut through the voices in her head and help her think clearly. So it was eight PM. It wasn't like she was going to sleep anyway, not with this news — or lack thereof — hanging over her head.

She tapped Denae's number in her phone. "Stan's not my dad."

"Um, didn't we already know that?"

"Well, yes, but I had some ideas." She filled Denae in.

"I'd tell you to let it go, but you haven't listened the last ten times I said it."

Sadie stared at the brew dripping into her mug and inhaled the sweet fragrance. As soon as the machine puffed air, she lifted the cup and took a quick sip. Ah. Better already. "Look, you know who your parents are. You don't get what it's like, not knowing. The doctors ask for my medical history, and I have no idea. Maybe I'm a walking time bomb and don't even know it."

There was a pause before Denae's voice came through clearer. "Is there something else you're not telling me? Any bad symptoms? Have you been to the doctor lately?"

"No. I'm not feeling that great, but it's not critical or anything. All they'll tell me is to lose weight, and that's easier said than done." Guilt tinged her conscience as she savored another sip.

"Sweetie, you—"

"Don't start." She knew it all. Get more exercise. Eat better. Blah, blah, blah. Her caseload was too heavy for that kind of nonsense. She was already working tens most days, and twelves were not uncommon. Bringing dossiers home on the weekends. Trying to find time to date a man who worked until after dark six days a week.

"It's because I care."

"Yeah, I know. It's just a really busy time in my life right now. Maybe once I make partner."

"Sadie. You've got a life to live in the meanwhile. It could be umpteen years before you make full partner. It takes time. My dad fast-tracked, and he didn't even have a life. He and Michelle were like ships passing out at sea. They barely saw each other for a decade. Trust me. It's not worth it."

She inhaled a big gulp of coffee and let it wash down. "Your dad's path was his. Mine's different. I'm in family law, not criminal prosecution." Hadn't she and Denae had this conversation before? Her friend hadn't dissuaded her then and wouldn't now.

"I know. I just hate to see you killing your health for unrealistic expectations. There's nothing romantic about that."

"Romance isn't everything."

"Says the girl who's going out with Mr. Gorgeous Hunk."

"He probably wants to have a pile of kids. Everyone in his family seems to favor large families."

Denae squealed. "You've talked about babies?"

"No. Observation only."

"Oh. Listen, I want to go on record as saying that who you live life with and how much you enjoy it are far more important than your salary and your job. I want to say your past doesn't matter nearly as much as your future. You, my friend, are in a most amazing place. I don't mean Bridgeview, though that's fairly decent. I mean you're at the beginning of a career that can be very rewarding if it doesn't swallow you whole. I mean you've got a great guy interested in you, a solid church to attend, and a dad who moved five hundred miles to live nearby. He may be awkward, but he cares about you. Just relax, Sadie. Enjoy the journey. Kick back and smell the roses."

Wasn't that what she was trying to do with the backyard renovation? "Because you are my oldest and dearest friend, I'll consider your words." It wasn't like she'd be able to prevent it at three o'clock in the morning with caffeine still surging through her veins.

"You do that. And I'll pray for you. I always do. You know that, right?"

"I know. I pray for you, too. Mostly I pray you'll move here."

Denae chuckled. "Not gonna happen. You can pray for my knight in shining armor, though. He seems to be taking his time slaying dragons elsewhere and forgetting he has a date with destiny over here."

"Maybe he's waiting for you in Spokane."

"You wish."

Yes. Yes, she did. "Maybe I should book a week off and go to Illinois. Want to come?"

"Illinois? Why on earth?"

"That's where my parents moved from. Maybe someone back there knows what happened."

"Hmm. I'll think about it, but I'm super booked. I don't think I could get away until fall, most likely. Give me dates as soon as you can, and I'll do my best."

Sadie gripped the phone more tightly. "Really? You'd do that for me?"

"After I said to give it up already? Yeah, I would. Only because you're one of my best friends and I know you'll do this with or without me."

Denae was right about that. The idea had grabbed hold. Maybe Sadie could get in touch with that cousin Lynda had mentioned a couple of times. What was her name again? Jackie something. She could just see Stan's face when she asked for Jackie's surname or, better yet, her phone number. He'd go apoplectic. Maybe she could figure it out without asking. Worth a try, right?

"Listen, I've got another chapter to edit before bed, and it's already nearly ten."

"Okay. Sorry for bothering you."

"Call anytime. Seriously. It takes my mind off how these fictional characters are falling hopelessly in love while there's no one here wanting to kiss me."

Maybe if Sadie could get her past figured out, she'd be able to be the woman Peter thought she was. He called her amazing. Kind. Sweet. She didn't feel like that woman, but she did enjoy his kisses.

CHAPTER 13

*P*eter threw himself into his work, like he had any choice. After an eight-hour day monitoring the controlled burn near the Idaho border, he threw on shorts and a T-shirt and dug into the soil of his gardens. It wasn't like Jasmine was sitting still, either. She worked equally long hours.

At least she'd finally seen reason and agreed they needed to hire someone to man the market tables, so now their cousin Landon and her teenage brother-in-law Jason had become the public face of Bridgeview Backyards. Hopefully that choice wouldn't come back to bite them.

Jasmine wasn't much of a people person. Peter didn't mind being at the market, but he was stretched too thin, and all he could think about was how thousands of weeds each grew an inch while he smiled and chatted with people in the sunshine, rearranging the veggies on the table as stock ran low.

They now had seven households subscribed to their box program. Thankfully these folks picked up from one of the two weekly markets. He and Jasmine had agreed that, for every ten subscriptions, they'd give one away to a needy family.

He'd hoped they'd be there by now, but Basil—

Peter jammed his spade into the soil. He and Jasmine never should have let her brother buy in from the beginning. They should have known he wasn't dependable, that he had a drinking problem, that he didn't truly share their vision. Basil's main priority had been quitting his laborer's job with the city. They'd been blind to his problems, thrilled that Basil wanted to invest and come on board. Thrilled he'd saved up a few thousand dollars at all. Must've been some kind of miracle.

Sweat poured off Peter's face. He dropped to his knees, wrapped his gloved fingers around a weed stem, and gave a sharp tug. It snapped. Great. He knew better than to yank on the things and break them off. A few seconds of patience, and he'd have been able to get most of the root, too.

How long could he keep blaming Basil for hobbling the startup with his stupid choices? The frustration and anger at his cousin were like weeds in the garden of Peter's mind. He did the same thing there, recognizing it for an unhealthy growth and snapping it off. But the root remained, so the weed regrew. Maybe Basil was just the face of Peter's frustrations, because he certainly wasn't the only one.

Sadie.

How could he be falling for a woman who cut him out of her yard? She didn't seem to find it incongruous. Bridgeview Backyards was Peter's heart, and she treated it like it didn't matter while kissing him in the moonlight. He wanted more kissing — and more than kissing — but his heart was leading him down the garden path, right out of the garden itself.

Peter yanked on another weed, snapping it as well. He was a fool. He'd gambled that she'd see to the heart of him and come to value what he was doing. He'd felt so close to that the night of the fundraiser, which was, after all, to benefit the homeless, to provide one of their biggest needs, healthy food. He felt she shared his vision. They were so close to aligning he'd assumed it would happen.

He'd kissed her.

He shouldn't have. Oh, he'd enjoyed it — and every kiss since — but he'd jumped the gun. He could see now that she remained focused on her own end game. And why should that surprise him? He did, too.

But how to extricate himself now? Under her public face, she seemed so needy. So fragile. If he broke things off, wouldn't it reinforce her low self-worth? She'd think he'd never appreciated the real woman inside, but only wooed her for access to her backyard. When she uprooted that, their relationship had no roots, either. And, yes, that had been in the back of his mind, especially at first. He'd joked about it to Wade and to Jasmine. But that didn't tell the whole story. He'd quickly fallen for someone who might be a believer but didn't have the same life goals.

He wiped sweat off his forehead with the back of his gloved hand and sat back on his heels.

How much had he prayed about the business situation before turning it personal? He'd uttered a few words to the Lord, but quickly found a perceived solution and run with it. A false solution that not only hadn't saved the business but was taking two hearts down with it... because it wasn't all about Sadie's property. His heart was definitely entangled.

Oh, Lord, what do I do now? I want to do what's right. Not just for me and for Bridgeview Backyards, but for Sadie. For the kingdom of God. I'm trapped in a forest of thistles and can't see a path out.

Peter dug out another weed, this time holding it up to see the roots down to the tiniest feathers. He'd left little of this one to grow again. He reached for another, continuing to pray while he worked. Tilting the face of his soul to accept a refreshing rain, a cleansing, a time of growth.

SOMETHING HAD CHANGED.

Sadie still saw Peter for a few minutes outside most evenings when they both finished work well into the evening. They still caught a movie some Friday nights. She still sat beside him in church and went to his parents' house afterward.

But something had changed. His kisses were less frequent, less passionate. He seemed distracted and exhausted. The man worked nonstop, but that wasn't anything new. She had no idea where he got his energy from. Sure, her hours were long, too, but she spent them at a desk, not hiking and digging and hauling things.

It was a Sunday afternoon in early June, and they'd been dating over a month. Dino and Ava bellowed at the Red Sox on television, while Peter sprawled on the sofa nearby, dead to his surroundings. Sadie extricated herself from beneath his head and made her way into the kitchen where Betta put away the last dishes from another delicious lunch. At least this Sunday Marietta was at one of her other sons' houses.

"Thanks so much for inviting me," Sadie said.

Betta smiled. "You're welcome. Would you like some tea? I noticed Peter sound asleep."

Tea in this household meant herbs Jasmine had picked and dried. Sadie could drink it to be polite. "That sounds nice." She slipped onto a tall stool at the kitchen island. She'd never gone one-on-one with Betta before. Maybe it was time.

Silence, punctuated by the ball game, stretched while Betta fixed two cups and settled on a stool around the corner. Sadie stirred in a large dollop of honey. Finally, her words spilled out. "Did your daughter ever consider giving up her baby for adoption?"

Betta angled her head and looked at Sadie. "You must see a lot of adoption from all sides in your line of work."

"I do." Sadie sipped the hot brew. "I sometimes wonder what goes into the decision."

"Dafne was so young when she got pregnant, only sixteen. The boy pressured her to have an abortion. No one would ever have to know."

Sadie looked down into the white china teacup in front of her. "That happens often."

"She decided last minute that she couldn't go through with it. The boy abandoned her at the door of the clinic when she refused, and she got on a bus and ran away."

"Oh, no."

"She found herself in Montana on Christmas Eve and

called my nephew Rob. You may have met Fran? She plays piano sometimes at church. Anyway, her brother lives there, and at the time he was dating a woman with two children. Bren, her name is. They're married now and had a baby just a few months ago. But then, Dafne needed that woman's wisdom. Needed to know God could forgive her and still had a plan for her life."

Which didn't explain the decision to keep the baby, although it sounded like that's what Dafne's mentor had done. Obviously, Sadie's biological mom hadn't had the same kind of mentor. At least she hadn't aborted. As unloved as Sadie felt at times, Lynda and Stan had taken her in, given her their name, and met her basic needs. All except for the one that consumed her for the past decade. The need to know her history.

She could hear Denae's voice in her head, even now. *Give it up. It doesn't matter.* But it was hard to let go. She'd tried.

Sadie glanced over her shoulder, but she and Betta were still alone. She lowered her voice. "Does Dafne ever regret not giving him up for adoption? There are so many families waiting for babies, and being a teen mom must be difficult."

"It was a hard decision a year ago. She changed her mind so many times it was like living with a yoyo." Betta shook her head with a small smile. "A hormonal yoyo. Even when she'd decided *for sure*, she still went back and forth. And, yes, there have been many times since Gavin's birth where she's wondered if she'd made the best choice for him. And for herself, of course."

"It can't have been easy going to high school pregnant."

"It wasn't. Gavin was born in July, so at least Dafne

didn't have to miss school for his birth. When classes resumed in mid-August, I took a leave of absence from the office to care for him."

Sadie shook her head. "Why would you do that? She's the one who chose to keep him."

"She's our child. Gavin's our grandchild." Betta chuckled. "The only one we have, you may have noticed. With today's open adoptions, we might still have had the opportunity to see him grow up, albeit at a distance. But when Dafne chose to keep him, Dino and I vowed to support her as best we could. It's been a fine dance some days, knowing when to step in and when to step back. She's still a child herself and will always be our baby girl. She picked a hard road."

"Giving him to another family would have been easier in many ways, I'm sure." That's what Sadie's own mother had done. Not only that, but she hadn't loved her baby enough to make sure the couple were cut out to be parents. Just gave her away and never looked back.

"At that stage, an easy road doesn't exist." Betta examined Sadie over the rim of her teacup. "Abortion might seem simplest at first, but evidence has mounted that the effects haunt the mother all her life. Adoption might often be best after life has been chosen, but it is a long way from easy, whether open or closed. There is a hole in the child's life, and also in the mother's."

"Definitely in the child's, but I don't know about the mother's," Sadie said softly, blinking back tears.

Compassion flowed from Peter's mother's eyes. "Do you speak from experience?"

Sadie's head gave a short, sharp nod against her will, just

as warm hands came to rest on both her shoulders. Peter. She closed her eyes and sank lower. He already knew — he'd met Stan, after all — but she'd never let the hurt show.

"Sadie." She felt the caress of his fingers and the warmth of his chest on her back. "Stan loves you. He cares for you."

"And Lynda tried. I know she did. But I've never known my mother." Seeing Betta, Sunday after Sunday, giving Dafne a hand with Gavin, had only made the hole larger. More gaping.

"Adoption in the Bible is depicted as the most beautiful thing," Betta said gently. "We were born in sin, but Jesus redeemed us. He didn't just save us and give us a reassuring pat on the shoulder as we went on our way. He adopted us into His family. We become sons and daughters, with all the rights and privileges that come with it. Imagine the magnitude of becoming the child of the God of creation. The heirs of the God of the universe. He becomes our *abba*. Our daddy. That's how powerful adoption is."

The gentle fervor in this woman's voice harpooned that truth deeper into Sadie's soul than it had ever been before. It had always seemed a mixed bag — the joy on new parents' faces in her courtroom as a child was declared legally theirs mixed with anguish for the child who, if anything like Sadie, would feel torn between two worlds for a lifetime.

Stan wanted her to give up the search. Was he wise to give that advice? She couldn't shake the thought that he was hiding something.

Why couldn't she rest in the biblical portrayal and let bygones be bygones?

CHAPTER 14

*C*ome in, come in!" Sadie held the door for Linnea and her long tubes of paper. Finally, she'd see what the designer had been working on.

Linnea gave her a quick smile. "I'm sorry it took so long. Some issues came up that took some time. You know how it is, I'm sure. Family always comes first."

Not in Sadie's world. Business was always the top priority. Unless... "I hope there wasn't a death."

"No, no. Nothing like that." Linnea hesitated. "I've seen you at church, so you might understand, and I know you've met my brother Dan. He became a Christian a couple of weeks ago."

"That's great." Although it didn't account for Linnea's time.

"He'd been living with this woman. She had a couple of kids before they hooked up, and then they had a baby together last year. Anyway, Dan knew their living arrangement wasn't biblical, so he asked Dixie to marry him."

"So... a family wedding? That's nice."

Linnea shook her head. "Dixie kicked him out, and Dan had to scramble for a place to live. He's bunking out with Alex and Peter right now, but he's a mess. He really loves her. Loves all her kids, not just his son."

Sadie opened her mouth then snapped it shut. What a mess some people made of their lives.

"I'm sure you see even weirder situations all the time in your line of work." Linnea swiped a tear from the corner of her eye. "Sorry. I promised myself I was done getting all emotional, but I guess I'm not over it."

This woman was a mess over her brother's failed relationship? Or more likely because he'd met the Lord. "It sounds like an awkward situation."

"Dixie's immature and selfish, and her mother is a bulldozer who never liked Dan and wants to keep the kids from him. It's a disaster."

The kind of disaster Sadie saw every day at the office. "Tell your brother to give Dawson and Banks a call and ask for an appointment with me. If he can prove he's the baby's father, I can definitely help."

"I don't think Dan wants to take her to court. And I doubt he can afford you."

"Maybe your parents could help?"

"Not a chance. They dislike Dixie as much as her mother dislikes Dan."

Sadie frowned. "Who's advocating for the children?" Because whatever mess the parents had made wasn't the kids' fault. Her heart went out to the little ones.

"That's the problem, isn't it? Kids always get the raw end of the deal. I admit it took a while for Mandy and Buddy — Dixie's older kids — to grow on me, but it isn't their fault their mom's a hot mess." Linnea took a deep breath and shook her head. "I'm sorry. That's not why I'm here. Can I roll these out on the dining room table for you to have a look at?"

"Sure." Sadie led the way, chewing on her lip. "Look, I'm not able to take on much pro bono work, but if Dan needs anything — if the children are suffering from this — please have him call. I'll do everything I can."

"Thanks. I'll let him know. For himself, he figures he deserves whatever Dixie dishes out, but the kids don't. He's worried she'll leave the kids alone and go out drinking — she's done it before — and someone will report her to CPS."

"That would be the best possible thing, wouldn't it? Child Protective Services exists to make sure the children are cared for." Sadie worked closely with case workers all the time.

"Not if they get sent into foster care and Dan loses contact."

"Wouldn't he be their first choice?"

Linnea unrolled the large papers and anchored the corners. "It's hard to know. He's not squeaky clean, either. It's really a muddle."

Sadie's curiosity was definitely piqued. "My offer stands."

"Thanks. I've got a few options for you to consider for your yard. This top one has everything you asked for and then some." Linnea traced a line on the paper. "This is the back of the house. This curved area is the patio. I was thinking red brick, but we can talk options. Over here..."

Sadie nodded and focused as the designer described the

elements, ticking each off her mental list. Linnea had even come up with a few ideas Sadie hadn't, but liked.

"Any questions about this one before we go on to other options?"

"I'd like to see more, but I don't see how they could be better than this. I think you nailed it."

Linnea offered a fleeting smile and rolled the top drawing out of the way to reveal the next. "This option gives you a lot of the same elements, but scaled back a little, both in vision and price."

Sadie studied the design, noting the smaller patio and a fountain rather than a waterfall from a built-up corner. Then her gaze zeroed in on the east side of the yard. "And this?"

"In case you were open to a compromise of sharing the space with Bridgeview Backyards, this design leaves their asparagus beds intact."

The nerve of her. "No. What's the third idea?"

"No point in showing it to you then."

Sadie rolled the offending design aside and studied the next for a few seconds. Linnea was right. She liked this one even less. Not only did it leave the asparagus but the berries and scope for more. She skewered the designer with a glare. "This isn't what I asked for at all."

"I know. It was just an idea, seeing that you and Peter are dating."

Anger bubbled up within. "Did he put you up to this?"

"No." Linnea sighed. "I'm always seeking the best scenario for everyone involved, much like you do in family law, I'm sure."

"This is nothing like my work." She didn't dare posit

that law was more important by far — although it was — because then Linnea would assume the back yard didn't matter. And it did. Was it really too much to ask for an oasis from the pressures of Dawson and Banks? That's all she'd asked of Ranta Landscaping. She certainly hadn't asked for compromises.

But what if she and Peter kept going out? Might they not eventually marry? She owned a home. He didn't. It was a natural thought he would move into this house with her. The house he'd always wanted. Was her insistence on a peaceful retreat unmarred by vegetables the reason he seemed busier lately? More aloof? His kisses shorter? Less persuasive?

She'd known it all along. Hoped she was wrong, but the evidence mounted that he'd only played along to see what would happen. She'd been the one to invite him to the fundraiser. He'd accepted because he was interested in the cause, not because he was interested in her.

Who would be? She was chubby. Awkward. Needy.

"There's one more." Linnea rolled away the well-beyond-compromise design to reveal another. "This one is a little less expensive than the first one due to the smaller water feature, smaller shade structure, and fewer plants. The patio is larger, so that's a slight additional upfront cost there, but ongoing upkeep will be lower due to less weeding and shaping." She hesitated. "And there's no space allocated to Bridgeview Backyards."

Sadie scanned it. "I'll take this one. What are the numbers?"

"She thought you put me up to it." Linnea stood by the front window, hands hanging as low as her woe-begotten expression.

Peter drove his hands through his hair. "I told you not to."

"I know, but I couldn't just let it go and pretend she was some random potential client I have no vested interest in."

"She'll be angry with me."

Linnea winced. "She's... not pleased."

He took a deep, shuddering breath. "What am I supposed to do now?"

"Face the situation? Peter, I hate to be the one to tell you this, but her reaction tells me she's selfish and not that into you."

"Nothing Jasmine and Alex haven't mentioned. I don't agree, but you're not alone in your belief."

Her voice softened. "What do you see in her? I'm not saying she isn't nice, or pretty, but what is it really that draws you to her?"

He'd asked himself the same thing a thousand times. Why, of all the women in Spokane, did he have eyes for Sadie? He worked with some really great women who loved the outdoors as much as he did. Some who went to other churches. There were even a few in the neighborhood, though his friends were snatching up the eligible women at a fast rate. There was Hailey North, co-owner of Bridgeview Bakery and Bistro, but... no. He'd known her since school, and there was definitely no spark.

What did he see in Sadie? Was it really only his desperation, either for a girlfriend or for the property next door? No. There was more. There had to be. "I see someone who's a conflicted mix of privileged and hurting. Someone who's a believer but whose roots aren't deep into her faith." That right there should be enough reason to back him up. "Someone who really needs someone to believe in her and see the best in her and love her."

"Do you love her?" Linnea's voice was quiet.

"I'm not sure. But it could happen." And then there was Nonna's prediction of their marriage. Nonna was rarely wrong about anything pertaining to her grandkids. But had he placed too much stock in her prophecy?

"Because I don't think she loves you back, Peter. At least, not now."

He closed his eyes, breathing in and out, absorbing her words. Praying. "I think you're right."

"Then what?"

Why did Linnea have to push? He didn't want to face it. He'd been shoving the disquieting thoughts under the surface for weeks. "It's not so easy, Linnea."

"Tell me."

"Now you sound like Rebekah with her counseling degree."

Linnea offered a half smile. "Then I'll be like her and wait for you to answer honestly and without deflection."

"Okay. Say I break up with her now. The first thing she'll believe is that I never did care for her and only wanted the yard."

Biting her lip, Linnea nodded. "And next?"

Wasn't that enough? "It's not true! I like her. A lot. But I'm not sure I could convince her at that point."

"What else?"

Peter forced his thoughts to line up. "She already feels

unworthy and unloved. She's not close to her adoptive dad and has no other family. Her only real friend that I know of lives in Missoula. I'm afraid breaking up with her would crush her."

"Is she suicidal?"

"I don't think so? But she holds a lot back. She's hard to read."

"And you don't want to be responsible."

He nodded. It sounded pathetic.

"You're a really good guy, Peter. It's no wonder she's attracted to you, but it's not enough. A real relationship, a solid marriage, needs a much stronger foundation than you two have. Ten years ago, you could get away with dating for fun, but you're what, twenty-eight? Things can turn serious very quickly, and I think you're in over your head."

Yes. All that was definitely true, other than the bit about him being a great person. Obviously, he wasn't so wonderful, or he wouldn't be trying to form an exit strategy from dating a woman who deserved better.

What a mess.

"One more thing."

Peter raised his eyebrows at Linnea. Hadn't she said enough already?

"What do you two have in common? She goes to church. That's terrific. Anything else?"

"She cares about people, especially kids in need. I know she's donated to Blessings Under the Bridge beyond the corporate fundraiser. She's a great advocate."

Linnea nodded. "That's super. I've heard really good things about that ministry." She hesitated. "She offered to help Dan out, pro bono."

Peter managed a grin. "See? Like that."

"Look, I'm not one to discriminate. I hope you know that. But Sadie's, well, overweight. Obese, even."

It was hard to deny she carried a few more pounds than many twenty-somethings. "She's very busy and doesn't eat right."

"That's what I mean. You're so active you manage to play three-on-three several evenings a week even after working two full-time jobs."

"Thankfully they got the lights fixed under the bridge, so the basketball court is better lit."

"You're deflecting again."

Drat. So he was.

"It's not really about her weight, Peter. It's that she doesn't seem to care. Know what's on her counter? Pizza boxes. An open carton with a couple of cinnamon rolls in it. Several pop cans. A coffee maker with a tower of over-sweetened pods. The lid was off her trash can in the back porch, and it's stuffed with a bunch of bags from drive-throughs." Linnea stepped closer, forcing Peter's gaze to meet hers. "There was a tied-off bag beside it. You know as well as I do that there are five people living in this house and, between all of us, we don't even generate half a bag of trash a week."

Peter took in a deep breath and let it out slowly.

"You can't tell me you haven't noticed this."

He'd noticed, all right. He'd noticed her pushing aside her vegetables in restaurants. She'd hesitated on their first date when the waiter asked if they'd saved room for dessert. He'd quickly said no thanks — it was his habit, after all —

but realized later she'd probably have asked for the dessert menu. Peter sighed.

"Trust me when I say it's not just because she's over-weight. The problem is that she's making super unhealthy choices. It's not just that she doesn't love you. She doesn't love herself."

CHAPTER 15

Sadie pushed open the door to Bridgeview Bakery and Bistro just after three. It was rare to get out of the office early but, once she had, the thought of chocolate peppermint cookies had lured her in.

"Good afternoon, Sadie!" called Kass North, one of the owners, from behind the counter. "Astrid will be right with you. Sorry, our one coffee maker is down — I'm waiting for the technician — and I just started brewing a pot in the smaller one."

Astrid? Since when did she work Wednesday afternoons? "Oh, don't worry about it." Sadie took a step backward, fumbling for the door.

But it was too late. Astrid appeared from the back, her eyes narrowing as she noticed Sadie. "What can I get for you?"

"I think she's after a coffee. I'm so sorry, Sadie. There's never a good time for machine failure, but if you've got five minutes...?"

But Sadie's gaze had locked on the display case where

several trays of baked goods rested. The sweet aroma tugged her closer. "I, uh... I'll get half a dozen of those cookies to go." She pointed at the chocolate peppermint ones. "I can make coffee at home."

"Sure. Astrid?"

The middle-aged woman stood with both hands on her hips. "You don't need them, girlie. We send the extras to a homeless ministry."

Sadie's face burned, but she braced her shoulders. "Are you denying me service?"

"No, she's not. Enough, Astrid. Please scrub the counters in the back."

The woman rolled her eyes, pivoted, and marched to the back.

"I'm sorry, Sadie. I don't know quite how to fire her since she's my fiancé's ex-mother-in-law. It's kind of complicated, but I apologize for her rudeness. She has no call to treat any customers like that. I'll definitely speak to her about it."

Which was worse, walking out empty-handed and angry, or accepting the apology and buying a few cookies? Astrid was right. Sadie didn't *need* them, but the homeless didn't, either. They were cookies, after all. An extra. A goodie. A delicacy she treated like a staple. The truth tried to hit her between the eyes, but she dodged. It had been a long day, considering how much anguish the Halburtons packed into their custody battle. Considering the time of the month.

Kass reached for tongs and began transferring cookies to a bag.

Sadie allowed it. She did need those cookies. She tugged out her wallet and insisted on paying, though Kass offered them as a truce. "It's great that you support a homeless ministry, though. I know several doing great work in Spokane. Blessings Under the Bridge is one of my favorites."

Kass smiled. "Mine, too. They serve a meal under the freeway by McClellan Street every Wednesday evening to over four hundred people. Since we heard about it, we started sending treats down. Volunteers from the church deliver them to their hub on Wednesday afternoon."

"I'm sure people appreciate it." If Sadie was supposed to feel guilty for taking some cookies from the homeless, it failed. The bakery needed paid sales to allow them to stay open and thus donate. She was actually helping. "Talk to you again soon." She turned to the door just as it opened.

Peter? Sadie hadn't realized he was a regular here.

"Hey there!" said Kass. "There are a bunch of boxes in the walk-in ready for you to grab."

He rocked from one foot to the other. "Sadie! You're off work early."

"For once, I am."

He grinned, that lopsided expression she'd grown to love. "Have plans? I'm dropping off the bakery's donation to Blessings Under the Bridge. Want to come along?"

Sadie should say no. She'd left work early because her head hummed and her muscles cramped tight from the stress of Jan Halburton's demands. She was so exhausted she could barely think, but it was nothing a caramel espresso and a bag of cookies wouldn't cure. At least temporarily.

He angled his head, grin in place, eyes warm. "I haven't seen you much this past week."

"I... sure, why not?" She could think of a hundred

reasons, but Peter was right. Much of it was her own crazy schedule, or the fact she might've been avoiding him since Linnea had been by with the design plans. She'd begged off Sunday, citing a headache, and stayed home with the drapes drawn. A candlelit bubble bath, a new book, and a pizza delivery had kept her very good company.

"We can either go from here and pick up your car after, or you can drive home and change while I load up. I'll pick you up there in fifteen?"

"Okay. Sounds good." She clutched her purse and bag of cookies and headed out. It wasn't until she was buckled in the car with a cookie to her mouth that she realized he hadn't touched her. Hadn't kissed her. Had he never done that in public? Hmm.

⌒ ‿ ‿

"HOW ARE THINGS AT WORK?" Peter glanced across the cab as he stopped at a traffic light.

She rotated her shoulders. "Busy. Stressful."

"Tell me."

"I can't. Client confidentiality."

He forced a smile. "I didn't mean names or details, just generalities."

Sadie grimaced. "Child custody in a divorce. They're making it ugly."

Peter turned toward the freeway. "That's really rough for the kids."

"Made worse because they're adopted to start with. To be *chosen* and then rejected is a double whammy."

"It's hitting too close to home?" Maybe this time she'd talk about it.

"At least I was an infant when I was adopted. These kids remember being shuffled around in foster care."

He merged, shifting the truck into fifth gear, before glancing at her again. Was this the time she'd finally open up a bit about her problems with Stan? Peter hadn't imagined anyone, adopted or otherwise, calling their parents by their first names until he met Sadie. "I imagine being a baby would make it easier."

"They never told me."

He sent her a questioning look. If they hadn't told her, how had she found out?

"It was Lynda's deathbed confession when I was sixteen."

Oh, man. He couldn't imagine.

"I lost my mother and my foundation in one go."

"But they still loved you as much as they ever had." He mentally kicked himself. "I mean, your dad... Stan..."

"They were older when I was born. When I found out about the adoption, so many things became clear. Why they didn't connect with me."

"I don't think it takes youth or blood for a connection." Peter scrambled for examples. "Like Dan Ranta. He's as broken up over losing his girlfriend's kids as much as over losing little Henry, his own son. He loves them the same."

Sadie shook her head. "Not possible."

"What, you're saying adoption is bad?" He couldn't wrap his head around her thought process.

"No, I've seen plenty of success stories, but some people really shouldn't be parents. I can't figure out why Stan and

Lynda adopted me. They were never like my friends' parents. Their lives rotated around work and social clubs. Church was one of those, it seemed. They weren't... affectionate."

Peter's parents might not have been perfect, but he'd never doubted their love. Even Dafne, who'd rebelled a couple of years ago, hadn't done it because she felt rejected. Smothered, maybe. He'd had Nonna to sneak him cookies, and he'd spent a lot of time at Uncle Ray and Aunt Grace's house, playing basketball with Marco, Basil, Alex, and Evan. They'd been the brothers he never had, to say nothing of his other cousins Rob and Tony. And Jasmine, the cousin nearest his age, was like another sister to him.

How would it be to feel alone and unloved? How could a guy break up with a girl who already felt rejected by those who'd promised to love her always?

Sadie gave a short laugh. "Sorry. Too much information."

"No. Not at all. I was just trying to process it. Why do you think they adopted you then?"

"It certainly wasn't for a trophy child, unless I failed at that so young they buried their hopes." She shook her head. "I even wondered if I was the product of an affair and taken in from guilt, but it turns out Stan and I don't share any DNA."

"You checked?" Peter's hands tightened on the wheel.

Sadie's chin came up. "I did."

He hated to follow the next thought. "And your mom...?"

"No one would have had to adopt me then. And her confession would have been quite different."

True. Peter passed a slow-moving eighteen-wheeler and pulled back into the right-hand lane.

"Where are we going, anyhow? I thought we were delivering food to a ministry downtown."

"Oh, didn't I tell you? Their drop-off center is in Spokane Valley. It's not that far." No more than his daily commute to the Fish and Wildlife office, a drive he couldn't wait to give up.

"I'm surprised they asked you to do it. Don't they know you've already got a lot going on?"

"You know what they say. If you want something done, ask a busy person." He shot her a quick grin. "Seriously, though, a bit of time was freed up when Jasmine and I hired our cousin and Nathan's half-brother to run the markets. Both guys are sixteen with newly minted driver's licenses, and they're doing a great job."

"Oh. I didn't know."

Because they'd spent so little time together. How could he even claim they were dating when they hadn't in nearly two weeks? She must feel the awkwardness as much as he did, or she wouldn't have stayed home from church and family dinner last Sunday. Was she distancing herself on purpose because he was?

Peter signaled for the exit lane to Spokane Valley as guilt overwhelmed him. He needed to decide whether to break up with her or go all-in... provided she'd let him. This limbo wasn't healthy for either of them. He glanced across the cab and took in her closed eyes and withdrawn expression. If she were someone like Jasmine with a strong sense of who she was, he'd pull out a book full of apologies and part ways. On the other hand, if she were more like Jasmine, he probably wouldn't be contemplating this. It was the weight of Sadie's need that was the problem, not the weight of her body.

◦ ◡ ◦

"LOOK, if he's not that into you, break up with him."

Sadie could envision Denae pacing her small Missoula apartment. "I'm not sure..."

"This isn't love, Sadie. It's not romance. Trust me."

Right. The romance editor had bared her fangs. "I know. It's just..."

"That you have a desperation to be loved. Is that it?"

It sounded pathetic. True, but pathetic.

"Look, we all have a longing for love. Haven't we talked about Maslow's hierarchy of need before? I know we have. Peter made a good start with those flowers and all, but he hasn't done that great lately, so he's likely having second thoughts. He—"

"He probably thinks I'm too fat."

Denae sighed. "Have you gained twenty pounds since you met him?"

Sadie glared at the phone. "No." Although she couldn't be sure, since she'd exiled the scale. And right now, she wished she hadn't polished off all six cookies while waiting for Peter earlier. She should've known she'd need a sugar infusion when she returned.

"If you weren't too fat on May first when he kissed you, you aren't too fat now."

"But you're saying I'm fat."

"Sadie, quit putting words in my mouth. Do you have

any idea how hard it is to be your friend when you get so down on yourself?"

She took a deep breath. "But... I know I'm too fat." She'd never spoken the words before. They hung, cold and isolated, pulsing in the air before gradually disintegrating.

Silence. Panic flushed through Sadie.

"Listen, I'm concerned about you. Yes, you're heavy, but we all have our hang-ups about food. The thing is, you're not healthy. You eat to take the edge off your emotions, like... like someone who drinks."

"You mean an alcoholic. You think I'm addicted."

Silence again for a long moment. "Are you?"

"It's not the same thing. Not at all. No one actually needs booze to stay alive, but we all need to eat. You could say we're all addicted to food."

"Sadie."

"What? I've got to go. Sorry I bothered you."

"Sadie Guthrie. Do *not* hang up on me. Do not go in the kitchen and rip open a bag of chips to try to drown out my words."

This called for something stronger, like Haagen-Dazs.

"Look, I try to keep my nose out of places it's not wanted, but you know what? You and I have been friends since we were little kids, and I actually love you."

Sadie bit her lip. They did have a long, shared history, and Denae was really the only close friend she had. "I know," she said softly. "I love you, too."

"Please understand that what I'm about to say, I say because of that love. Okay?"

Sadie braced herself. "Okay."

"You're out of control, girlfriend. You need to love yourself before you can love Peter or any other man. And when you love someone, you care about them. You meet their needs if you possibly can. You strive for the best in them."

The words filtered into Sadie's mind and trickled through to her soul.

"Love yourself, Sadie. Advocate for yourself the way you do for kids you meet in your office. Cut the junk out of your kitchen and out of your thinking. Find a Christian counselor. Decide you're worth it."

Sadie swallowed hard. "Are you done?" she asked hoarsely.

"Depends on if you hate me yet."

"I don't. I couldn't ever."

"Okay, one last thing. Don't take this on because of Peter. It has to be for you, or it will all come apart at the first sign of trouble."

That made altogether too much sense. "Thanks."

CHAPTER 16

Sadie pulled into her driveway at only quarter past three, heaving a sigh of relief. The Halburtons had had their day in court. Jan had trusted Sadie to get custody for the children, and she'd lost. She hated losing, but the opposing counsel had presented solid, overwhelming arguments on the father's behalf, and the judge had awarded him custody.

She shook her head as she exited the car. As if either of them were the real parents. Imagine adopting kids from foster care and then inflicting divorce on them. Those poor kids.

And poor Sadie. She couldn't remember when she'd been this exhausted before. She'd poured her heart and soul into this case for weeks. Losing stung. She'd told Cordell she was taking the rest of the afternoon off. Yeah, she should have gone back to the office after court. It wasn't like Jan Halburton was her only case right now, but she had to take care of herself, too. Denae said so.

Too much stress. She rounded the corner of her house.

When would she get the peaceful oasis she needed back here?

Then her gaze landed on Jasmine kneeling in the garden bed, rubbing her fingers together as she shifted down a shallow trench.

"Excuse me?" Sadie's voice sounded sharp, strident, even to herself.

Jasmine surged upright, turning as she did so. "Sadie! I thought you were at work. You surprised me."

"I came home early." Which should be obvious enough. "What are you doing?"

"Um, seeding radishes?"

Sadie's hands found her hips. "I believe I made it quite clear that your business was to remove all the growth, not plant more."

"Well, yes, but—"

"I also don't believe I left any room for questions."

Jasmine's eyes narrowed as she mimicked Sadie's pose. "But we have until Ranta Landscaping starts work here."

"Only to harvest, not to sow more seeds."

"They grow quickly and will be ready to pick long before mid-July."

"That was not our agreement." Sadie would definitely remember if Peter had asked. "Which is now null and void. If you're going to be in my yard, start digging up those asparagus plants."

Jasmine's eyes shot darts. "It's the wrong time of year. It will kill them."

"That is not my problem. I would have been entirely within my rights to demand immediate removal and was more than fair allowing you to harvest the crop, which, from what Peter has said, is ostensibly complete."

"Sadie, look—"

"No. Did Peter put you up to this?" Sadie braced herself against the realization that the past two minutes had effectively ended any hope of rebuilding that relationship. Well, Peter would likely be glad, since he'd seemed to avoid her lately, anyway. He'd figured out she wasn't lovable, so there was no longer any point in trying to pretend she was.

"You can't blame him for this." Jasmine leaned forward. She might not be tall, but she wasn't a pushover. "We had a big order for radishes, and this space was going to waste. I didn't see what it could possibly hurt."

"You were counting on me being at work and never noticing."

By Jasmine's silence, she knew she'd nailed it. She grasped the railing to the back porch as her legs weakened. If she couldn't have her lounge chair set up out here yet, at least she had a comfy sofa inside with a fleece throw to snuggle in. And a cat, if Anastasia deigned to be touched. Sadie felt cold despite the warm June day. Chilled right through, actually.

What had she done?

Something she should have done from the beginning. She should never have let Peter's intense blue eyes weaken her resolve for carrying through her original plan. If she'd stayed focused, she might not have failed Jan Halburton, either. She'd done too much daydreaming about Peter's square shoulders and handsome face.

She stared at Jasmine. "I don't see you digging up those plants yet."

"Let me tell you something about radishes. They may seem hard and bitter when they're raw but, if you cook them, they are soft and mild." Jasmine's eyebrows rose. "It's when you put something in hot water that you find out what it's *really* made of. Think about that. It's a life lesson." She yanked her trowel out of the dirt, stalked through the gate — latching it with a clank — then strode up the path behind the house next door. Of course, *she* could hike the steep angles of Bridgeview without a second thought. She was skinny. Fit.

Unlike Sadie.

Well, whatever. Sadie might not have a cute husband or an entrepreneurial streak, but she also wasn't obsessed with herbal tea and vegetables. Who cared about radishes, anyway? They were off-the-chart disgusting. Normal people didn't even think of them as vegetables.

Sadie climbed the few steps to her backdoor and into the kitchen before letting out a long breath. It must be the battle within her that sapped all her strength. Was she going to regret laying down the law with Jasmine? Because it would rapidly trickle down to Peter, if it hadn't already, and that would be the end of what had once seemed a promising romance. Before she'd had another look in the mirror.

Denae said she needed to get healthy for herself, not for Peter. Well, Peter was out of the way now, but was she really worth it?

She inserted a fresh pod of caramel espresso into the coffee maker and pressed start.

"YOU DID *WHAT*?" Peter drove his hands into the hair at his temples. "I can't believe you did that."

"Me?" Jasmine stepped closer, right into his space. "What about her?"

"Jas, you knew she was a little touchy."

"Listen to yourself."

"You are totally missing the point."

"I think you are."

Peter strode into the kitchen, poured himself a tall glass of water, and gulped it down, as much to gather himself a moment to think as to hydrate himself. He turned back to the living room where Jasmine paced in front of the window and Nathan straddled a chair, gaze toggling between them. "Why did you think planting next door was a good idea?"

His cousin whirled to face him. "Because we have a big order for radishes for that event in July and that is the only one of our garden beds with enough room. How was I supposed to know she'd come home early? How was I supposed to know she'd be so stinkin' touchy?"

Peter inhaled as slowly as he could manage and matched the exhale. "You should have asked."

"You... or her?"

"The landowner." He'd thought about Sadie's yard, too, when that order had come in yesterday. But she'd been so distant lately, and he didn't know what was going on.

"I thought maybe being the landowner's boyfriend's cousin would make it okay." Jasmine had lowered her voice. "Besides, you know the saying. It's easier to beg forgiveness than ask permission."

Peter shook his head. "Unless it backfires."

"Well, it usually works just fine."

Nathan chuckled. "Says the middle child with a pile of brothers."

Jasmine shrugged. "It's part of my life experience, so whatever. And how was I to know there was trouble in paradise?" She glanced at Peter. "You never told me."

"Like you confided every step of your emotional journey with Nathan to me as you were going through it."

"Touché." Nathan nodded.

"Whose side are you on?" Jasmine glared at her husband.

"This is between you and Peter, a Bridgeview Backyards thing." He held up both hands. "I'm merely an observer, but I will say you each have made some good points."

She swung back to face Peter. "Besides, I did you a favor."

"I'm not entirely sure how you figure that."

"She's selfish. She thinks of no one but herself, and I think you're well rid of her."

"Jasmine..." warned Nathan.

The words cut through Peter's anger, draining off the frustration and every other emotion. He turned away, leaning over the sink and staring into the backyard. Neat rows of raised garden beds filled the space, lush with growth. This had been his dream for several years. He'd worked hard to make Bridgeview Backyards a reality, sharing his vision with Jasmine and Basil. Managed to survive the catastrophe of Basil's drunk driving conviction, jail time, and eventual departure from Spokane. Now he'd lost the house next door, including its yard and the woman who lived there. The woman he'd tried to convince himself he was falling in love with.

Jasmine was right. Sadie was selfish. But there was more

to her than that. He'd seen tantalizing glimpses of a thoughtful, generous nature, someone who truly cared about children's needs and those less fortunate. She was a beautiful woman who knew what she wanted, warring with a hurting soul who craved love and acceptance.

Was he the right man for Sadie? Did he only feel sorry for her or want to keep access to her yard open? Or was there something else, another option, where he actually loved her? There'd definitely been hints of that possibility, but it had been hard to be certain amid the weeds of the other conditions.

And now it was all moot.

Yeah, he needed to talk to Sadie and confirm that he heard her words, all of them, including the fact that it was over between them. There wasn't any way to romance through the way she'd shredded Jasmine. Maybe his cousin *had* done him a favor by pushing the point, so Sadie's true colors were revealed before he got in any deeper.

He should probably feel relieved.

He didn't.

THE KNOCK at the back door and the ding of an incoming text combined to wake Sadie out of what had apparently been a deep sleep, filled with dreams of radishes with happy faces bouncing around in boiling water.

She blinked and pushed herself to sitting. By the light angling in the living room window, it was mid-evening. Four hours of sleep should refresh her more than this. Her gaze fell on a half-full mug of coffee. That didn't happen often.

She picked it up and took a gulp, wincing at the chemical taste in the cold brew. Yuck. Definitely better hot.

Another ding reminded her of the unread text, but she ignored it in favor of the door. She paused when she came around the corner and saw Peter through the window. No. She wasn't prepared for this.

He glanced down at his phone, gnawed his lip, looked around the yard.

Sadie filled her gaze, filled her memory banks. Had she been too hasty with Jasmine? Should she eat crow? No, she couldn't. Eating crow meant eating radishes. It meant more indecision, more awareness of the gulf that had formed between her and Peter. It was better this way, although not the method she'd have chosen had she been thinking straight.

She moved toward the door on leaden limbs.

He glanced up at the movement and riveted his gaze on her.

Those eyes. He was such a nice guy, really. She tugged open the door. "Hi."

"Are you okay?"

Sadie blinked. Not what she'd expected him to say. "I'm fine."

"You look pale."

"I said, I'm fine." Her curls were likely a mess. Why hadn't she stopped in front of a mirror before coming through the kitchen? "I had a difficult court case this afternoon and came home early. Just in time to catch your partner planting."

His gaze was steady. "She shouldn't have done that."

"You're absolutely right." Sadie steeled herself. "It's time to dig it all out, Peter."

He stared at her, unflinching. "The asparagus?"

"Everything."

"It sounds like you are talking about more than gardens." He toggled his finger between them. "Are you talking about us, too? Pretending there's no attraction between us?"

"Attraction isn't enough. We're too different. We don't have common goals."

Why didn't his facial expression twitch in the slightest? If she was carving out his heart, shouldn't he plead that he loved her? Her suspicions were true, then. He didn't really care. "I think the biggest appeal for you was the garden space. I let myself believe there might be more for a time, but I shouldn't have been blinded. It's over, Peter."

"There *was* more."

Sadie noted the past tense. "You don't need to pretend. I'm a big girl." She winced, but why not go for it and cement the deal? She swept her hands down her body. "A really big girl, as it turns out. But I can handle rejection. I've been dealing with it my whole life, one way or another, so what's a little more?"

Oh, she was lying through her teeth. She didn't want rejection, but it would have come any day now, anyway. She'd only taken the shortcut. This way, she held a little control over the depth of the pain.

She could pretend, anyway.

"Sadie, I can't change your past. I can't even change your perception of it. All I can say is, God understands."

She clenched her jaw. How could he toss God in here like this?

"I'm not rejecting you. You're taking it out of my hands, but the needs in your soul are not something any man can fill. God is the only one who can give you comfort and everything your heart craves. I've been praying for you, Sadie, and I'm not going to stop." He pivoted and marched down the steps.

He was halfway across the yard before she found her voice. "When are you going to dig up your stuff?"

"On Saturday."

Good. She'd make sure she wasn't home.

CHAPTER 17

I'm morbidly obese. I'm going to die."

"You're *what?*"

Lying on the sofa, Sadie held her phone away from her ear at Denae's typical shriek. "I saw the doctor today. It was so humiliating."

"Why did you go to the doctor? Tell me more."

"I, um... haven't been feeling really well. I came home from work early a couple of days ago and kind of crashed."

"What kind of crashed are we talking about here?"

Sadie gnawed her lip. "I was so exhausted I couldn't stand up. I had a nap, and you know I never do that. I haven't felt like myself since then." Might also have something to do with the confrontation with Jasmine and then Peter.

"Good for you, going to the doctor. Did she run any tests?"

"My blood pressure is sky high, and my blood sugar is in a bad range, too. She ordered other tests, and I'll get the results next week."

"Oh, boy. What does your dad say?"

Sadie glared at Anastasia, since Denae wasn't in the room. "Why would I talk to Stan about my health? He's no help. Not when the doctor asks about my family's medical history, and I don't have a clue what it is."

"Maybe... if he actually knows something, this will push him to reveal it."

"I thought of that, but I doubt it. What does he care?"

"I think you're doing the man a great disservice, Sadie. He didn't sell his house in Cannon Beach and move to Spokane because he doesn't care. He'd lived there forever."

"Only since I was a baby. Which reminds me about that trip to Illinois. I'm thinking late August."

"I'll see what I can do. Listen, Sadie?"

Here came the other barrel. "Yeah?"

"Give your dad a break. Call him. Tell him what's up."

Sadie forced a laugh. "And here I thought you were going to tell me how to be as skinny as you."

There was silence for a long moment. "You don't want to be. Trust me, I have my own hang-ups."

"Are you—"

"I don't want to go there. Just know that every woman has her own set of insecurities, okay? Everyone."

Sadie had cut Linnea and Peter's family out of her life along with Peter. How pathetic was it that she didn't even know that many other women at all? She cringed deeper under the fleece throw that had become her constant companion in the past few days. It was crazy her only close girlfriend lived a couple of hundred miles away... and amazing Denae even pretended to put up with her. No wonder Denae refused to move here.

"Oh, one more thing."

Sadie rolled her eyes, but she'd asked for it by phoning Denae. "Yes?"

"Have you talked to Peter about it?"

Sadie winced. She'd somehow talked herself out of whining to Denae about that situation since it happened. "He's not in the picture anymore."

"Not in what picture? Did he break up with you just when things got rough? That's mean, Sadie. Just plain nasty."

"No... it was me. Remember, you told me to."

"Not exactly. Besides, I thought you'd come to your senses and see what a great guy he is."

"He is a great guy. He just happens to have made some life choices I can't get behind."

"Uh... like what? Because I'm having trouble imagining any huge flaws."

"His obsession with gardening. Vegetables."

"Sadie..."

"No. I know you like them, but I don't, and he's crazy about them. And it's not just that. It's my whole backyard thing." She filled Denae in and skimmed over the later confrontation with Peter with as few words as possible.

"Girlfriend."

Sadie sighed. "What?"

"Veggies are not one of those things you just get to take a pass on. Your body needs them. Needs them like you need water and air. You said the doctor gave you a stern talking to. Did she recommend a nutritionist or counseling? Because if you're going to get well, there are going to be vegetables in your future."

Ugh. "I don't even know where to start. Not with asparagus or radishes, that's for sure." Why didn't tomato sauce and pineapple on a pizza count?

"I've heard good things about Green Acres Farm in Idaho. I think they offer programs on nutrition."

"I can't take time off work." Not after losing a couple of days already, and the week she'd asked for later in the summer.

"Maybe they have weekend stuff. Look into it. They're Christians and have been running a farm school for — man, I don't know. Five years? Ten? They have all kinds of cool programs."

"Sure." Anything to get Denae off her back. But wasn't that reverse thinking? Was she really going to lie back and accept a death sentence? Morbidly obese sounded horrible in the extreme. Sure, there were women fatter than her, but that was a lousy excuse. She had to deal with her own concerns, not someone else's. And her issues were staring her in the face.

Denae ended the call, and Sadie glared at the cat.

The doctor had used words like *at extreme risk for heart disease* and *at extreme risk for diabetes*. There might have been more, but she'd tuned out about then. Wasn't that enough?

What had Jasmine said the other day? It's when you put something in hot water that you find out what it's *really* made of.

Sadie didn't want to face the mess she'd made. She wanted to keep blaming Stan and Lynda and God. She wanted to blame genetics for her weight. So long as she didn't know her bio mom was skinny like Denae, she could do that, right? Maybe she didn't want to delve deeper. Continuing to barricade herself might be for the best.

Except that morbidly obese people were apparently at higher risk for dying young, and it seemed too depressing to simply sit back and wait for that to happen. She'd taken charge in college. She had a rewarding career. She could take control of things if she cared enough. Surely, she cared enough about her health. Her life.

And what about God? She'd been making her spiritual life to be all about ethereal things like goodness and kindness and charity, avoiding the discipline side of things. Who liked denial? Self-control? Not her. Not anybody.

But, there came a time.

Besides, Peter was praying for her.

She thumbed on her phone's web browser and tapped the microphone. "Green Acres Farm," she enunciated, and waited for the search results to roll onto the screen.

LINNEA LOOKED up from the drafting table when Peter came into the room. "Did you find a place to plant your radishes?"

"I took over a back corner of Nonna's yard, but she sure gave me a talking to. She's adamantly on Sadie's side."

"What? Why?"

"Oh, you weren't at church the Sunday they met. Nonna announced — to everyone within listening distance, I might add — that Sadie was the girl I'm going to marry, and a little breakup isn't enough to dissuade her." Might as well argue with a stone wall.

"Your grandmother is a piece of work."

He lifted both hands as he shook his head. Hard to deny.

"You're going to be able to meet the order, at least?"

"I think so, yes. The radishes might not be as big as we'd hoped on harvest day, but they'll be as big as they are. Not much else I can do besides hope Nonna doesn't drown the seeds."

Linnea grinned. "She's too experienced a gardener for that."

"You'd think. But she's determined to help me save face with the client, and you never know what's going on inside her head."

"Until she blurts it out."

"There's that." Peter poured a glass of ice water from the fridge dispenser. "What are you working on?"

"A big project for a couple over in Glenrose. Pretty sure they want to show off how much money they have."

"You'll be happy to take your share?"

Linnea scrunched her nose. "I feel guilty doing it. Not taking their money, exactly, but helping them spend it on stuff with no lasting value."

He dropped onto Alex's sofa. "I hear you."

"What are you going to do about Sadie?"

"There's nothing to do." He leaned forward, elbows on his knees as he twisted the glass in circles. "She made it pretty clear she suspects my motives and she's done with me."

Linnea grimaced. "She's such a hurting soul. Logan and I have been praying for both of you."

A phone rang, and Linnea reached for hers from the side table by the window. "Eden! How are things?"

She listened for a moment, a frown furrowing her brow. "Dixie's not there? When did she leave? ... No, Dan's mowing Ridleys' yard this afternoon. I'll come down and see to the kids ... Thanks for watching out for them and calling me."

Peter finished his water and raised his brows as Linnea set the phone down. "What's up?"

"Eden heard Henry crying and went next door when he didn't stop. Mandy said her mom's been gone all day. There were empty pop cans and cracker boxes in the kitchen, and the baby stank." Linnea surged to her feet and stuffed the phone in her hip pocket. "That Dixie. I don't know why she keeps having kids when she obviously doesn't want to be a mother."

Peter scratched his ear. "And you're going to...?"

"Go down there. Eden changed the baby, but someone needs to feed those kids a good meal, clean that house, and stay there until one of their parents returns. Dan needs to file for custody."

"I thought he had."

"He didn't think he'd be able to get it for the older two since they're not his kids. Plus, he works six days a week, and Dixie doesn't. Obviously, she doesn't do anything at all. He didn't want to rock the boat and have her cut him right out of the kids' lives."

"And now?"

"Guess we'll see." Linnea strode over to the door, grabbed her purse off the hook, and marched out the door. A few seconds later she returned and grabbed a key ring.

"Might need to transport children," she muttered darkly, and disappeared again.

A few seconds later Peter heard her car start then pull away. He took a deep breath and let it out. This whole adult thing left a lot to be desired. A broken relationship. A baby sister with a baby of her own. Friends who'd made shambles of their lives. A chosen career that depended on the fickle weather, which always seemed too hot or too cold or too rainy or too dry... to say nothing of the yard owners and their personal problems.

But some people in this city had bigger difficulties. He thought of the night he'd been able to get away and volunteer at Blessings Under the Bridge. Nearly four hundred people had come for a hot meal that night. Young and old. Even some children.

He buried his face in his hands. "God, this world is a mess. People are a mess. We all need you so much. There's wars and famines and persecution and natural disasters and poverty and abuse and... the list goes on and on. I don't even know where to start praying. To start helping."

Although, he'd already started helping. With their tenth subscription, he and Jasmine had chosen a family in the church to bless with a box of fresh produce weekly. Norris Trenton's job had recently been made obsolete, and the couple had five kids under thirteen. The tears of gratitude in Trudy's eyes last week had been all the payment Peter needed.

Dan's truck pulled into the drive. The door slammed and heavy boots clomped to the door. Dan exploded through it, a dark scowl on his face.

Looked like Linnea had gotten through to his cell.

Dan marched down the hallway to the bedroom he'd been camped in for a few weeks and returned a moment later with a duffle bag over his shoulder. He glared at Peter. "If that's how she's going to play the game, then she can be the one to move out of the house, not me. I'm paying the rent, anyway, and I'll make sure there's someone around to watch the kids when I'm at work. Uh... do you know anyone?"

Peter rose and cuffed the other guy lightly on the shoulder. "Do what you have to do. You know we're standing beside you, praying for you."

Dan's eyebrows wobbled. "Yeah. I guess this isn't anything I didn't expect, but I hoped it would be different. You know?"

"I know. You could try my sister Daf, if you don't mind her bringing Gavin along. Not sure she's up for watching four kids under the age of five full-time, but she might be willing in a pinch."

"Her kid is only a couple of months younger than Henry, isn't he?"

Peter thought back. "Yeah, I think so."

"That's a lot for someone who's no more than a kid herself. Although apparently, it's even too much for their biological mother. Maybe I'll see if Dafne can bail me out for at least a few days while I try to find someone more permanent." Dan drove his hand through his already messy hair. "This is a nightmare."

"God—"

"Yeah, I know. And I'm not going back on it. I wouldn't even if I thought it would make a difference, because Dixie and I were headed for this cliff even before I decided Jesus was my answer. That decision only tipped us over a little faster."

"I'm really sorry, man. Wish I could do something."

"You're already working two jobs." Dan turned at the door. "Your girlfriend, though. She told Linnea she'd help me if she could. Do you suppose it's worth checking out?"

Peter winced. "Ex-girlfriend."

"Aw, man. Sorry."

"Try her, though. She knows all about these situations. She really has a soft spot for kids who are being shuffled around."

"I'm done with that uncertainty. I'm going to fight for Mandy and Buddy, not just Henry. They don't even know their own fathers, but they know me, and I've done right by them." He jerked his head in a nod. "Dixie can take that to the bank. I'm calling her out."

The door slammed behind him, and Peter sank back to the sofa. "Lord? Like I was saying, the messes are everywhere."

CHAPTER 18

*S*adie lowered herself into a lounge chair in Stan's backyard. She wanted a patio just like his with some shade, sweet flowers, and a water feature. If she hadn't been so determined to snag a heritage home, she might've found this one before he had... and saved herself the trouble of fighting over her own yard with Peter and Jasmine.

Peter.

She pushed him back out of her mind. What was done was done.

"I'm concerned about you, Sadie." Stan's brow furrowed as he handed her a diet cola then settled into a chair nearby. "Are you okay? You seem tired..."

His words trailed off. Sadie could guess what he'd thought better of saying, that it was the first time in forever she'd sought him out. Which was true.

"It's been a rough couple of weeks, actually." Even though she'd come by to apprise him of her situation, she still didn't want to. She took a deep breath. "I've had some health difficulties."

Stan's eyes sharpened on hers. "Oh?"

Sadie offered a shaky laugh. "Oh, nothing that losing a hundred pounds wouldn't cure." Possibly. Hopefully.

"Like what?"

"Exhaustion. High blood pressure and cholesterol markers." She stared at a hummingbird feeder. "To name a few."

"I'm sorry to hear that." He seemed about to say more but didn't.

What, she'd taken the wind out of his sails by saying she knew she was heavy? Had that removed the power of his disapproving looks in the past?

She raised her chin. "Go ahead. Might as well say what you were going to say."

Stan shook his head.

"Of course, the doctor asked for my family's medical history and, as always, I had nothing useful to say."

"What difference does it make? They'll give you medication to manage your symptoms regardless."

"It makes a difference to me. Did my mother die of heart failure at a young age? Did all the women in my family struggle with weight? Who was my mother, Stan?"

"Sadie, focus on yourself. On your own wellbeing, not some mystery person. This obsession isn't healthy for you." He took a sip of his root beer.

"You knew her, didn't you?"

Stan sputtered in his drink.

"You probably still do." Why she added that last bit, she had no idea, but the words popped out at his obvious shock. Sadie struggled to her feet and stared at the man she'd thought was her father for sixteen years. "Deny it."

He stared back, his mind obviously scrambling for answers by the twist of his mouth.

"Never mind. I'd hate for you to perjure yourself. I'll see myself out."

"Sadie, wait." Stan parked both hands on the arm rests of his chair and levered himself upright.

"Why?" She turned, one hand on the latch on the side gate. "So you can tell me again how you provided a good home and education for me? So you can tell me again how thankful I should be? Thank you, Stan. Thank you for rescuing me from... oh, wait. I have no idea what you rescued me from, do I? It's hard to follow that train of thought into the station. We'll just leave it as a generic thank you."

Amidst all the other good stuff, the doctor had advised Sadie to lower her stress levels. Right, she'd get right on that as soon as she got home, and her hands stopped shaking enough to scoop out some Haägen-Dasz. Except she wasn't supposed to do that anymore, either. Well, pounding out a five-mile run wasn't going to happen. How was a girl supposed to destress? The woman she'd talked to at Green Acres Farm — Sierra, her name was — had said they'd talk about things like that when Sadie came for the weekend. It couldn't come soon enough.

"Your mother and I cared for you a great deal."

"What does that even mean?" Sadie glared at Stan. "I care for my clients. If that's the best you've got, no wonder I felt insecure all my life."

He rubbed his hand across his forehead. "Loved, okay? She loved you. I still do."

She couldn't remember when she'd last heard those words,

awkward as they were. Still, she'd pushed him into saying them. It wasn't like he truly meant them. "I've booked a week off late in August." Drat, she hadn't meant to tell him this.

"That's nice." His voice perked up. "I hope you're going somewhere relaxing."

"Illinois."

Stan's jaw dropped as he stared at her. "Illin... why would you go there?"

"I thought I'd look for my mother, but maybe you could tell me if she still lives anywhere near Naperville."

"Sadie, don't..."

She wasn't an attorney for nothing. She could tell when she'd uncovered the truth even when the evasion continued. "You can tell me what you know, or you can let me figure it out by myself, because I'm going to. Think of all the *stress* you can save me."

It was a mean dig. She knew it even as she said it, but she felt like her entire life was in free fall, like Alice tumbling down the rabbit hole past maps and pictures and empty jars of orange marmalade. Only Sadie was pretty sure it wasn't a gentle landing in wonderland awaiting her at the eventual bottom, but something more like a crash with broken limbs and a mangled heart.

Stan looked away, seeming to weigh his options, his gaze sliding across hers for a brief instant. "It's not my story to tell."

"Are you trying to tell me you are not the Stanley Nathaniel Guthrie whose name is on my birth certificate? If you're not, we're looking at a criminal investigation. And if you are, then you *are* one of the players in this story. Not the only one, I'll grant you that, but it's definitely your story, and you know more than I do about it."

He shook his head.

The last wisp of her patience evaporated and a flare of anger surged to take its place. "Goodbye, Stan." She marched out the side gate and down the sidewalk to her car. Tears flooded her eyes, but she drove around the corner before stopping to let them flow, once again, over the gift Stan could have given her but didn't.

Old patterns died hard. She'd meant to tell him about the breakup with Peter, about her upcoming trip to the Idaho farm, about the struggle to find God in her new reality. Instead, she'd slid straight into her old rut of accusations and aloofness.

Why did she always feel the need to protect herself? And even in that self-preservation, to inflict pain on others before they could do it to her?

～ ᴸ ᴸ

"READEEEEE?"

Peter dodged around Logan as Alex fired the basketball at him from the sidelines. He'd been so busy with two jobs and a girlfriend he'd missed far too many practices with his cousins, and Hoopfest was only a few days away now. Yeah, it was a busy weekend for Bridgeview Backyards, too, but sometimes a guy just needed a break. All work and no play made Peter a dull boy. His reflexes were certainly off if even Logan could out-maneuver him.

He no longer had a girlfriend. Bitter pill that a stupid

backyard garden had squashed what might've become a promising relationship.

Peter feinted and leaped, flicking the ball through the hoop with a satisfying swish.

"Peter's the man!" yelled Evan, but only seconds later, Nathan scored a point for the other team.

Back and forth. Block, pass, shoot.

The Santoro Bulldogs had made it to the top five percent in their division a couple of years back. The team had morphed some since Basil had moved away. They'd had to combine forces with the younger guys, but Peter figured Evan was better than Basil, and they stood a decent chance of advancing even further. Logan, Nathan, Wade, and another guy were fielding their own team in the challenge.

Peter was ready to ignore reality for two days of sweat, shoes skidding on pavement, and mingling with thousands of other teams from around the world on the forty-five blocks of courts closing streets downtown. It was insanity, and he loved every minute of it.

He faked a pass, dribbled between Logan and Wade, and jumped for a shot. *Swish*. He tried for a victory dance in the air but, as he landed, his foot tangled with Nathan's, and they both crashed to the concrete.

Peter rolled to bounce to his feet, but the pain shooting up his ankle dissuaded him. Alex grabbed his hand and yanked him upward, but Peter yelped at the jolt.

"You okay, man?" hollered Evan.

Another swish told Peter the other team had scored, but blackness danced at the edge of his vision. He took a step toward the edge of the court and crumpled again.

"Halt!" bellowed Marco then leaned over Peter. "What happened?"

"Ankle." Peter gritted his teeth.

His cousin probed the spot gently with warm hands, and pain radiated up Peter's leg. "Ouch. Hurts."

"Doesn't look good, but I can't tell if it's a break or a sprain. Should get some ice on it and see how it does."

A circle of faces leaned over him. "Need a ride to the ER?" asked Logan. "I stopped to play on my way home from work, so I've got the truck."

Broken or sprained? What did it matter which it was? It definitely wasn't a little twist that would be better by morning. Hoopfest started in two days, and either would take longer to heal. Peter felt like bashing his head against the court, as though pain at both ends of his body would help to even it out.

"Just take me home. Please."

"You sure, man?" asked Nathan. "That's gotta hurt."

"I ran into you." Peter was still seeing stars. "You okay?"

Nathan shifted from one foot to the other. "Fine. Caught my elbow a little, but it's okay." He stretched his arm and retracted it a couple of times. "See?"

"Good." Peter closed his eyes for a second, but his ankle still felt like a band of dwarves attacked it with axes. Good? Nothing about this was good. Not jumping on a spade to turn over new ground. Not hiking up the river to monitor fish stocks. And definitely not three-on-three for Hoopfest.

"Should I just take him home and get ice on that, or haul him to ER?"

Peter tried to focus on Logan's voice, but it came from a distance and seemed accompanied by a swarm of bees.

"Let's get him in the truck. Marco, grab the other side. We've got you, Peter."

He felt himself being lifted upright and bit off the gasp of pain that brought him sharply awake again. Could a sprain really hurt this much?

"ER it is," said Logan. "Dude, you have your ID with you, or do we need to grab it from the house?"

"Wallet's in my backpack." He got the words out between clenched teeth as the guys tried to ease him into the cab.

Alex set the pack into the backseat then rummaged in it. "Ah ha. Here you go." He passed the wallet over the console to Logan. "Meet you there."

"No." Peter leaned back on the headrest as the wooziness took over again. "I'm not dying." Although he couldn't be entirely sure.

"Hey." Alex squeezed his shoulder. "You can't get rid of us that easily. I just need to jog home and get the car, and we'll be on our way."

Wade leaned around Alex. "Praying for you, man. See you soon."

One of the guys shut the door as Logan started the engine. Peter braced his good foot on the floorboards. This wasn't going to be the most fun ride he'd ever had.

CHAPTER 19

Sadie wasn't sure what she'd expected as she pulled into the driveway just out of Galena Landing in northern Idaho, but this wasn't it. Yes, there was the gorgeous timber frame building, its roof covered with solar panels as shown on their website, but she'd been instructed to come further onto the property. A pair of small round buildings sat on the hillside above the school. At least, they had to be buildings by the windows and doors, but she'd never seen anything like them.

She passed a duplex as a large stucco house came into view beyond. On one side stood barns and corrals and a garden larger than she'd ever imagined, while on the other, houses made of logs, timbers, and another one of curving stucco seemed to be part of the hillside. A playground with half a dozen kids climbing on it sat in the shade of several large trees.

Sadie parked beside the biggest house. "Lord? I'm nervous. Maybe I should just go back home and try to figure this out by myself. It's the day of the internet, after all." Also, the days of whackos who touted a thousand ideas as the only ones worth listening to. She could spend a lifetime and more money than she could earn in that timeframe and be only halfway through the list.

Denae had recommended these people as down-to-earth and knowledgeable. The down-to-earth bit seemed true by the mix of chickens and children.

She was here now. She might as well hear what they had to say. If it all sounded too woo-woo she didn't have to stay, right?

A woman who looked to be in her mid-thirties emerged from the house and waved as she crossed the deck and came down the steps to the parking area, carrying an African-American toddler on her hip.

Sadie levered herself out of the car. "Hi. I'm Sadie Guthrie. I believe you're expecting me?" She held out her hand.

Instead she was enveloped in a hug, the giggling child squished between them. "Oh, I'm so happy to meet you! I've been watching for your arrival. I'm Sierra Rubachuk." Sierra held Sadie at arm's length and beamed before hugging her again. "We're going to have such a good time together."

When was the last time she'd been spontaneously hugged? Sadie couldn't even remember. That had been one of the best things about dating Peter, come to think of it. Just touch.

She managed a smile around the tears that threatened to flow. "Pleased to meet you. And who is this lovely little lady?"

The little girl grinned but leaned on the woman's shoulder.

"My daughter, Zoey." Sierra waved a hand toward the playground. "You'll find a lot of children around here. My friends and I bought this farm ten years ago, and I assure you we never expected to find God's perfect men for us way out here! But we did, and there's been a bit of a population explosion since."

"Your husband must be black."

Sierra shook her head, still smiling. "Nope. He's blond with blue eyes. We were unable to have children, so we've adopted four. Three of them are half-siblings." She blew kisses on Zoey's neck, and the toddler giggled. "Zoey's our youngest, unless God sends us another."

Adopted *four*? Across racial lines? No time like the present to start offloading her issues. "I was adopted, too, but I didn't find out until I was a teenager. At least your children will always know."

"Oh, that must have been rough."

"You have no idea." Perhaps she was doing the older woman a disservice. Who knew what the remainder of her experience was?

"God knows." Sierra gave her another squeeze then motioned toward the house. "Come on inside. We'll get your things later — we've assigned you the first duplex for the weekend. But, everyone will be gathering for dinner soon, so you can meet the rest of the team. Be warned! There are a lot of us, and it gets noisy. To say nothing of confusing to remember who belongs with whom. Don't worry about it, though. I'll probably be the one spending the most time with you."

"Okay. Thanks." Sadie beeped the car locked as she walked toward the house, not missing Sierra's quick grin. It was a habit. Sue her. No one would likely steal anything out here in the middle of nowhere, but there were a pile of kids on that playground, and she didn't want to take a chance.

Sadie stepped inside the house and blinked at the sudden change in lighting. A table longer than she'd seen anywhere, anytime, blocked her path. Two boys who looked to be about five laid forks and knives in front of each chair. To the right, off the end of the table, sat a spacious living room with several leather sofas and large chairs visible in the light from the expansive windows.

On the other side of the table, an eating bar with several tall stools marked the edge of a busy kitchen. Two women waved to her.

This was going to take some getting used to.

"Come on around," Sierra beckoned. "If we'd known how big a tribe we'd amass, we might have built a bigger main house. We definitely wouldn't have put the table in front of the front door."

"Everyone eats together? Like, all the time?" Surely that couldn't be true. The table held over twenty settings. Just the thought of cooking for that many people day in and day out made Sadie shudder. She couldn't even handle cooking for one.

"I know. It sounds crazy, but it works for us. Everyone cooks on rotation, and the kids all have chores, too." She nuzzled the toddler. "Even the little ones, right, sweets?"

Whatever a two-year-old could do to help, but the boys setting the table seemed to be managing. One of them carried a pitcher of water now, biting his lip with full concentration as he stretched to set it on the table.

Sadie wanted to give the kid a hand, but she resisted.

None of the other adults in the area seemed to think it was almost too much for the little guy. He flashed her a grin and dashed back into the kitchen.

"Allison, Claire, this is Sadie." Sierra pointed out which was which, and they greeted each other. Allison reminded Sadie of a slightly older Denae, tall and thin with long dark hair.

"Is there anything I can do to help?" Sadie pressed her hands to the peninsula counter, out of the melee. The aromas of seasoned pork and fresh, yeasty bread filled the space.

"We've got it." Claire shot her a smile. "We never put anyone to work the first day."

"Which means look out tomorrow!" Allison carried a pottery bowl of potatoes to the table. Several more bowls followed. Sadie cringed inside at the sight of green beans then two kinds of salad. She'd have to eat some of each to be polite. Everyone would notice if she didn't.

Right, she was on her way to a newer, healthier self. One who adored vegetables. Yeah. It was going to take more than a little self-talk to break down her barriers.

PETER HOBBLED around the house on his crutches. The place was far too quiet. His cousins had recruited their other cousin Dominic, Aunt Winnie's son, who'd shown up from Seattle for a few days, and roped him into taking Peter's place. A slight charge for the substitution, and the Bulldogs were off and running without Peter. He couldn't fault them for not wanting to forfeit the team fee and their part in the Hoopfest frenzy, even though it was raining.

Being stuck in the house drove Peter crazy, but he was smart enough to know he'd never navigate the crazed crowds downtown even as a spectator, let alone drive himself with his right ankle broken. And, if he could, parking spaces were at a premium anywhere near the blocked streets marked off with the half-courts and portable hoops, signifying the world's largest three-on-three competition.

"Lord, why?"

If he had a penny for every time he'd uttered those words, let alone thought them, in the past two days, he'd be a rich man. Wasn't he trying his best to do what God asked of him? He did his job, or at least he had until this stupid injury. He'd be unable to drive with a cast, so he'd need to catch a ride with Wade for weeks of office duty. Punishment enough.

He honored God and his fellow man by growing vegetables. Not only were he and Jasmine helping to fill a real need for busy families with their subscription service, they planned to tithe a bonus subscription to a family in need for every ten sold. Just two weeks ago, they'd delivered the first box to the grateful Trenton household. And they were struggling enough without Basil. How was Jasmine ever going to manage the next month or two until Peter was back to useful? Two teenage guys were only going to be so much help, and Ranta Landscaping kept Logan and Linnea busy.

And then there was Sadie.

Peter drove his hand through his hair as he stared out

the front window overlooking Bridgeview and the river down below. A light rain drizzled down.

Was it so wrong to want a thriving business, a home, a wife, health? What was he being punished for?

Yes, he'd gone about it with Sadie all wrong. They'd started off on the wrong foot and never quite regained their balance. The fact they both wanted her backyard for completely different purposes, had always loomed between them, an irreconcilable difference.

She was so prickly.

But had he been any better? Had he really treated her with the love and care God wanted him to shower on the woman he was dating?

Speaking of prickly, was that his grandmother trudging up the steep hill, rainbow-hued umbrella in hand? She might be seventy-nine, but that didn't stop her from staying active and involved in the community. Involved in her grandkids' lives. He watched her make her way up his street then into the driveway before he swung his way over to the back door and opened it wide. "Nonna! Welcome."

"Pietro." She folded the umbrella before squeezing his cheeks with her work-worn hands and kissing the air on either side. "What is this I hear from your mamma? The young people say to break a leg, but I think they don't mean it literally. It is supposed to mean good luck for actors, no?"

He hugged her close, the fragrance of the summer rain emanating from her. "I wouldn't call this good luck. Have a seat, Nonna. Can I get you some iced tea?"

She chuckled, pointing at his crutches. "That would be a trick, no? I will help myself and get some for you." She reached into the cupboard for glasses and filled them from the jug in the fridge.

Some host he was. The broken ankle affected every ordinary task. He clumped over to the sofa and took a seat, accepting the glass Nonna proffered before she settled into a straight-back chair.

"I see they play three-on-three without you. In the rain."

Peter grimaced. "They do." He wouldn't even mind the drizzle. "Good for them Dominic came early for the Fourth of July and that he's been playing in Seattle."

"It does his mamma's heart good to have him home for a week."

Peter was sure that was true. Aunt Winnie seemed to be doing okay since Uncle Al's death last September, but it had to be difficult to have her eldest across the state where he was in medical school at the University of Washington. Peter hoped to catch up with Dominic while he was home on this brief visit.

"Does God have your attention now?"

Peter blinked at Nonna as a protest formed on his lips. Didn't God always have his attention? But he bit back the words before he uttered them. Yes, he did desire to do God's will, but he'd been so busy his devotional life had become rote.

"I have worried about you, Pietro. So busy always. Running here, running there, doing two jobs, playing three-on-three, having a girlfriend. When is there time for God?"

All of that was gone, or at least on hold. Both jobs. Hoopfest. Sadie. He'd been so swamped the past two weeks he'd barely processed the end of their relationship. Peter released a long breath and looked at Nonna. "It's been a busy season." To deny it would make him a liar.

"What has God been teaching you lately?"

He took a sip of the iced tea, stalling for time, trying to think of something. "Jasmine told a story the other day that has stuck with me."

Nonna nodded, watching him. "Tell me."

"She'd read about a woman who was complaining about her life, so full of problems that she didn't know what she was going to do. Everything was a mess." Peter grimaced. "I couldn't relate at the time, but I can now."

"What did this woman do?"

"Well, her father took her into the kitchen, filled three pots with water, and put them on to heat. Then he added something different to each pot. In one, he put a few eggs, in another, coffee grounds, and in the third, potatoes." Peter thought back. "After a while, the father turned off the burners and indicated the contents of each pot and asked her to analyze them. The eggs were hard-boiled, of course. Completely changed from the raw, runny things they'd been before. The coffee grounds had seeped into the water in their pot, making a rich brew. And the potatoes had softened and tenderized."

"And the point of the story?" Nonna asked after a moment.

"We all face adversity... hot water. The egg was fragile before and became hard and rubbery. The potatoes were the opposite, once hard, becoming soft. And the coffee grounds changed the adversity itself into something completely new."

"That is a good lesson. It is up to us how we respond. Which one are you, Pietro?"

"I like boiled eggs as much as the next guy, but in the context of this story, that's not what I want to become." Certainty took hold. "The other choices are about equal, don't you think? To be made into something new, something better and more accessible?"

"You speak of the coffee, *si?*" She held up the iced tea. "Or it could be said of tealeaves. And what of the potatoes?"

"They're like radishes. Boiling water tenderizes them and takes the bitterness out of them. Makes them sweeter." *Lord, let me be like a radish.*

"Into each life some rain must fall," Nonna mused. "Are you familiar with the poetry of Henry Wadsworth Longfellow?"

Peter blinked. "I've heard the name, and that line is familiar."

"The poem is called 'The Rainy Day.' Look it up, Pietro. I do not recall all the words. Longfellow laments the days that are dark and dreary but concludes his ballad with the famous words: *Be still, sad heart, and cease repining. Behind the clouds is the sun still shining; thy fate is the common fate of all. Into each life some rain must fall; some days must be dark and dreary.*"

Had words like these comforted Nonna when her husband had passed away? Or possibly more recently when her youngest son had died?

"The thing is not to waste the dark and dreary times, Pietro. We are called to hold fast in the storm, knowing that our God is faithful and will never let us go. Remember your namesake when he decided to step out of the boat and walk to his Master on the stormy sea? He was a brave man, Peter the Rock, to even venture there. He only needed to keep his eyes on Jesus."

If God had allowed this storm to strengthen Peter's focus, well, he had plenty of time to contemplate for the next week or two.

Nonna peered out the window. "The rain has stopped for the moment, and the sun struggles to appear. I will take this moment to walk home."

He hugged her. "Thank you for coming. I didn't know I needed you." A moment later, as he watched her make her way down the sidewalk, closed umbrella swinging by her side, a faint rainbow spanned the valley.

Wasn't that just like God?

CHAPTER 20

After a breakfast of scrambled eggs stuffed with so many veggies Sadie gave up trying to pick them out, she accompanied Sierra and Jo back to the duplex. Guess this was it, then. She'd paid for counseling, and she was about to get her money's worth. A panicked prayer erupted from her mind, followed by a calming sensation. She knew she needed changes. Knew she needed to make different choices. Knew something had to give. Nothing these two women could say to her would come as a shock, and Sadie had the option to ignore all their advice and return to Spokane and her old way of doing things.

Back to the threat of diabetes and heart disease looming over her. No, thanks.

But... could she actually make the changes? It wasn't like a one-time thing where every extra pound would be magically erased. No, it was going to take time. She'd have to decide ten thousand times. It would be easier to give up now than put herself through all that just to give up later.

"Shall we have a seat at the table?" invited Jo. "Sierra

told me a bit about your story, and why you'd like to discuss things with a nutritionist. That would be my specialty."

The woman was the same petite shape as Peter's cousin Jasmine. Had she ever had a passionate love affair with pizza and ice cream in her life? There was no way Jo could understand.

No. Sadie was going to trust. Listen. She settled on one of the padded chrome chairs at the table while the other two women took seats at either end. "I was always the pudgy child, and when I hit puberty..." Sadie let her hands sketch her body. "I'll admit it. I eat my stress."

Jo nodded. "What do you eat?"

No hiding the truth, not that it was any more possible than an elephant hiding behind a telephone pole. "Fast food. Coffee. Sweets." Basically, the three food groups.

"And how do you like your coffee?"

"I buy the caramel espresso pods in bulk, but I can make do with a few other flavors if I run out." It never happened.

"Tell me about your relationship with God."

Sadie blinked. "Um, I was raised in a Christian home. We were in church every time the doors opened. I was eight or nine when I asked Jesus into my heart."

"And how did it go after that?"

She took a deep breath then exhaled. "I've never stopped believing, but I guess it isn't relevant to my life most of the time. I mean, I go to church. I read the Bible sometimes and pray when I think of it. I figure God gave us all brains and expects us to figure things out."

Sierra leaned forward. "Are you aware that God loves

you passionately and personally? He has a purpose for you, you alone, not just a generic one for all people."

"Yes?" Sadie responded with hesitation. "I mean, yes, I've heard those words, but I came to talk about my health. About losing weight."

"As believers, our faith is foundational to everything else," Jo said. "We're holistic beings. Every part of who we are is entwined with all the other parts. Don't you agree?"

Hard to argue with. Sadie nodded slowly, feeling like she slid down a slippery slope.

"Jo's right," added Sierra. "It's when we fully embrace our position in Christ that we can address the other areas of our lives. We realize our bodies are God's, and we adore Him so much we have a deep desire to offer Him a temple that's the best it can be."

"That's great. Really, it is. I'm not sure how you can help, though." Sadie nodded at Jo. "Do you even weigh a hundred pounds?"

The smaller woman met her gaze straight on. "One ten."

Before Sadie could claim her victory, Sierra spoke from the other side. "I was about thirty pounds overweight for a number of years. Like I suspect is your case, Sadie, some of it was depression and feelings of low self-worth. In my case, some of it was linked to my inability to conceive. Even Gabe's steadfast love wasn't enough to keep me from overeating sweets, especially."

Okay. Thirty pounds was something. It wasn't a hundred, but it wasn't nothing, either. Sierra still carried curves, but without obesity. "What did you do?"

"I claimed victory in Jesus' name." Sierra met Sadie's

gaze. "Not once, but many, many times. I claimed His love. I claimed His healing in my life. I claimed His power."

"Something else that's relevant here," Jo put in. "Sierra didn't walk this by herself. She, Claire, and I bought this farm together about ten years ago, and we pledged to communicate and to lift each other in prayer. The others joined us later and made the same promises. It's almost like a marriage covenant between our six families."

"I'm not sure what would have happened if I'd had to go it alone," Sierra admitted. "I tried for a few months, and I ended up in a very bad place emotionally. Do you have a community around you, friends who can offer accountability and just be there for you?"

Sadie shook her head, closing her eyes. "No. I just moved to a new neighborhood a few months ago, and I'm really busy with my work." Peter had that with his family and friends. That sense of belonging was one of the things she'd envied most.

"You're in Spokane, right? What part of the city?"

"Bridgeview—"

Sierra's squeal cut through Sadie's voice. "My brother lives there! Maybe you know him and his wife, Jacob and Eden Riehl? They live across from the riverfront walkway."

"I don't think we've met, but I could be wrong. I started attending the neighborhood church a couple of months ago, but I haven't gotten to know that many people. Just the people next door."

"From what I've heard," Jo put in, "it's a great community to get plugged into. I'm sure you can find friends and accountability partners there."

Sadie winced. "I think I got off on the wrong foot. I

dated one of the Santoro men for a bit, but we had some differences of opinion. And that clan makes up half the neighborhood, I think."

"Okay, well, for now, you can phone me every night." Sierra squeezed Sadie's hand. "But part of your homework is finding a friend who lives nearby and can become part of your daily life."

Counted Denae out, then. Sadie eyed Sierra. "Phone you every night and talk about what?"

Jo set a notebook on the table and flipped it open. "We're going to set some daily goals and celebrate each achievement."

Oh, boy. Sadie was going to hate herself for asking, but she had to know. "What kind of goals? Because I think you're scaring me."

The other woman grinned. "We'll start slow. Don't worry. But I also sense that you're very concerned about your health, so we won't go *too* slow."

If that was supposed to be comforting, Jo had failed. "Right."

"This first week, we're going to have three daily goals. First, we've got scripture readings to meditate on. Sierra will email them to you every morning."

Sadie nodded. So far, so good.

"Then, we want you to go for a thirty-minute walk every day. It's fine if you need to drive somewhere to do it. I know Bridgeview is really hilly, though you might want to try the riverfront path. Manito Park is lovely, or there's a nice path on the north side of the river through the Kendall Yards area. Don't get in a rut but check out different areas. We'll build up from the half hour later. No need to push hard in week one."

At least she didn't have to hike up the hill under the bridge. If she could choose flat sidewalks, she might survive this. "Okay. The other goal?"

"Write down every vegetable that you eat. A cup of raw leafy greens counts as one serving, or a half cup of something cooked. We'll work our way up to eight or ten servings a day but, for this week, just record reality."

The words exploded from Sadie's mouth. "But I hate vegetables."

Sierra offered a sympathetic smile. "That was the old Sadie. The new one adores them. She revels in all the new flavors and textures and variety. She loves all the minerals and vitamins and fiber and how strong they make her feel. The new Sadie thinks veggies are the bomb."

That was taking mind over matter a bit too far, but at least no one had taken away her French fries or espresso. Yet.

THE GUYS STREAMED into the house, laughing and talking, bringing the smell of rain, sweat, and pizza with them. Peter's nose twitched as he tucked his crutches under his armpits and made his way into the kitchen. "How'd it go?"

Evan slung an arm over Dominic's shoulders. "Dom's soft. We won one and lost two."

"You're out then?" Peter wasn't sure how that made him feel. They'd worked so hard, but Dominic hadn't played with the locals regularly for five or six years now. A double elimination tournament moved quickly.

"Out," Alex confirmed. "That last game was close, though. We nearly squeaked through."

Peter looked behind his cousins. "Where's Marco?"

Evan wrinkled his nose. "Thought he needed a shower and some of Daria's home cooking more than he needed Bulldogs' camaraderie."

Alex set two boxes of pizza on the counter while Evan reached for plates.

Dominic gave Peter a sheepish grin. "Sorry I let you guys down."

"I think I did that first. Thanks for filling in for me. Hope you had fun?"

"Yeah, I'd forgotten the Hoopfest vibe. I spend too much time hitting the books." The younger guy shrugged. "Guess it showed out there today."

Alex dumped three pieces of pepperoni pizza on a plate and pointed to the living room. "This is for you, Pietro. Go sit down."

"You don't have to wait on me."

"Yeah, Alex." Evan grinned. "Let's see how he manages pizza and crutches at the same time."

Some days he'd like to wipe the omnipresent smirk off the young buck's face. "Okay, fine. I need help. Does that make you feel better?"

"Shut up, Ev." Alex strode by and set the plate on the sofa's side table. "Don't be a bigger pain than you have to be. I'll get you a can of pop if you like?"

"Water, please."

A few minutes later his cousins wolfed down pizza,

guzzled pop, and relived their day on the courts while Peter leaned into the sofa and let the stories wash over him. He hadn't missed a Hoopfest since he'd been about ten, growing up through the various youth brackets until he and the guys had settled into the standard adult division. They'd entered in the family division once, but the competition was hotter in standard, and they liked it aggressive.

Still, he couldn't blame Marco for choosing to go home to his wife after a day of hard play rather than hanging out with these young guys. Peter felt not only wounded but old. He had six years on Evan, after all. Should he hang up his Bulldogs jersey permanently? Naw, not when he remembered those men in their seventies who fielded teams every year.

Maybe this was just one more area of life where he had unrealistic expectations. Add it to romance, business... everything.

Nonna was right. With all this extra time on his hands, his primary focus should be getting his priorities right. He'd been scrambling for months, maybe longer. It was time to do the grown-up thing, analyze his life, and make some changes.

CHAPTER 21

*H*ave you talked to that hunk next door yet, girlfriend?"

Sadie stared out her kitchen window at the smooth dirt where there used to be rows of asparagus. "No. There isn't really anything to say."

"I can think of a few things, like 'I was an idiot,' and 'I'm sorry.'"

She sighed. She hadn't even seen Peter coming or going since she'd returned from Green Acres a few days ago. "While those things are true, it's too late."

"It's never too late until one of you is dead."

"Wow, you're full of cheer, aren't you?"

Denae clucked her tongue into the phone. "You forget who you're talking to here. I read romance for a living. I happen to know that true love can conquer anything, but you might need to eat humble pie."

Pie of any sort sounded amazing. She'd take it with lemon meringue filling, thanks. Did the lemons in it count as fruit? Probably not. Sadie became aware that her friend was still talking. "Pardon me?"

"I said, he's probably waiting for you to make the first move."

Heat swelled up Sadie's face. "Because I was so forward and asked him out in the first place?"

"No?" Denae sounded confused. "Because you're the one who went ballistic and ordered him off your property. It's nothing that can't be overcome, mind you. Because true love—"

"I don't think true love is involved here." Sadie thought back through their short relationship. "I mean, it started promising, but it faded quickly. I think he regretted getting involved." The shorter kisses and days without contact had been a clue. "I'll only look desperate if I go over there now."

"Hmm."

Sadie could picture Denae tapping her chin. "Look, don't worry about it, okay? Seriously. I've got some junk of my own to work through right now. It's not fair to try to date Peter or anyone else while I'm such a disaster. And it's gone nuts at the office again."

"How are things going with Sierra?"

"Good. Every morning she sends me a scripture and a devotional with guidelines for prayer. That's been really helpful for getting my head screwed on straight."

"Like what?"

"Well, there was that one about whatever you eat or drink, do it to the glory of God. I'd never thought about eating being a spiritual act, if you know what I mean."

Silence for a moment. "And what else?"

"On my lunch break, I've walked around the block a few

times most days. It's not very relaxing, but it's a start. I worked through lunch on Tuesday, though."

"Have you thought about getting a treadmill or elliptical? Then you could do it at home before or after work."

"Hmm. I might think about it." If she did, wasn't that like committing herself to the new regimen? It would sit in her house, taunting her with yet another unkept promise. Unless she actually used it. Unless she actually did commit. Wasn't her health worth prioritizing? But that brought her to Sierra's third assignment.

"So... how about the veggies?" asked Denae.

Yeah. *That* assignment. At least for this week, it was only to record, but she felt like a loser reporting zero servings for several days straight. Sierra hadn't sniped at her admission, but the guilt was still there. "I had a bite of broccoli last night."

"Go you!"

"How do you eat that stuff? It has a vile odor and it's mushy and disgusting."

"Oh. Well, it doesn't have to be. Must have been at some cheapie diner."

"It was, but still."

"No, it's great raw. You can even have it with a dip. Or it's delish roasted in oil with some good seasoning."

Roasted? How on earth would that improve it?

"Or in stir-fries, cooked just until it's barely tender. Mmm. So good."

Denae was going to have to work harder than that to convince her.

"I'D OFFER TO HELP, BUT..." Peter sat on the sofa at Wade and Rebekah's, his right foot elevated.

Rebekah flashed him a smile as she set a bowl on the table. "It's fine. I can still manage, and Wade will be downstairs in a minute." Peter's friend and co-worker had taken the toddler upstairs to change her diaper before dinner.

"I feel like a lump on a log and about as useful."

"You think *you* feel like a lump on a log?" Rebekah raised her eyebrows and ran her hand over her large belly. "I can barely reach around this child. I feel like he's going to be born bigger than Olivia is now."

Peter chuckled. He was pretty sure he was supposed to. "When are you due?"

"In about ten days." Rebekah glanced at the staircase. "I hope he comes sooner, but it would be good if he waited another couple of days until Wade is done picking the cherries in the permaculture forest."

Another way Peter felt useless. Last year he'd given Wade a hand. Basil had still been around, working with Bridgeview Backyards. Not only was Basil out of the picture now, so was Peter, leaving Jasmine with most of the labor. Yeah, he'd spent a few hours crawling around in one of the gardens this week, dragging a basket behind him, plus they'd hired the two teen boys for as many hours as they could afford. So much for making a profit. So much for Peter being any closer to giving notice at Fish and Wildlife. He was going to go totally stir crazy stuck in the office for the entire summer instead of in the field.

A grimace on Rebekah's face caught his attention as she turned partially away, gripping the back of a chair tucked under the table. Peter narrowed his gaze as she took a few quick breaths. "Rebekah?"

Wade descended the staircase, blowing raspberries against his daughter's neck. Olivia giggled. Then the foot-steps ceased. "Rebekah?" Wade set the little girl on the floor, and she ran toward Peter.

Peter scooped her up with one hand, but his attention remained riveted on his friends. Wade put his arm around Rebekah and said something to her in a low voice. She gave a quick nod but kept her grip on the chair. Wade cast Peter a worried frown then turned back to his wife. A few seconds later, Rebekah shuddered then straightened. Wade swept damp blond hair from her forehead and kissed her temple gently.

Even Olivia bouncing on Peter's chest wasn't quite enough to distract him from the tender scene playing out across the living space. Something important unfolded before him. Not just the fact that Rebekah seemed to be going into labor, but the wholeness he sensed in their rela-tionship.

He'd known Wade a long time. They'd worked together at the Department of Fish and Wildlife for over a year before Rebekah had taken a temp position counseling in this school district. Wade had never mentioned the woman who'd run from his proposal four years before that but, when she was back in his life, he'd been determined not to let her get away again. God had done spectacular things in both their lives, and their marriage stood as a solid testa-ment to God's gracious intervention.

The thought struck Peter like a blow. God was in the business of happily-ever-after. Why else would He have sent

Jesus to a sin-filled planet, to certain death? It was only because of love. Because of a hitherto unfulfilled longing for that relationship to be complete. Full circle. Reciprocated.

Did God care about the romantic happiness of each person He'd created? Watching Wade care for his wife in this exact moment seemed to indicate yes. Then there were Peter's contentedly married cousins. Marco and Daria. Jasmine and Nathan. Rob and Bren. Other friends around Bridgeview, like Logan and Linnea, and Jacob and Eden. It was likely they all had moments where it seemed the storms of life would never end, but a few raindrops didn't stop them from believing the sun would shine again. They hoped in it, believed in it, strove toward it.

Olivia smeared a slobbery kiss across Peter's chin, her wispy hair dragging through it, her blue eyes peering into his. "Peetah?"

"Have I been ignoring you, baby girl?" He tickled her until she collapsed on his chest in giggles, but half his attention remained on the toddler's parents.

Rebekah came into the living area with a measured pace, her hands cradling her belly. "Peter, I don't know how to tell you this..."

He smiled at her. "The little guy decided it's time to make his appearance?"

"Quite possibly. I had a few random contractions this afternoon, but this one seemed considerably more intense. We'll keep an eye on the timing for a bit now." She gave him a bright smile, though the lines still showed on her face. "Either way, supper's ready, so let's sit up to the table. Come on, Livvie. Daddy will help you."

Wade wolfed down a few bites as though unsure when

he'd eat again, but he kept an eye on his wife, who twirled a few strands of spaghetti on her plate. Peter wasn't all that hungry himself. Too much sitting around, too much to worry about.

Rebekah gasped and swayed, closing her eyes. Wade knelt by her chair so quickly Peter didn't even register his movement. "Eight minutes. I think we need to go up to Deaconess. Is your bag packed?"

She managed a nod, and he dashed for the stairs.

Peter opened his mouth and snapped it shut again. The helpless feeling that had clung to him all week closed in tighter.

Wade skidded to a stop beside his wife again. Then he seemed to notice Olivia. His gaze shot to Peter. "Oh, no."

The helpless feeling swelled.

"Fran was going to watch Livvie, but they're out of town for the weekend. The baby's early." His gaze ricocheted between Peter and Rebekah.

"I can stay with her for a bit. At least she can walk, because I'd have a hard time carrying her."

"Are you sure? I can call someone else, but—"

Groaning, Rebekah clutched her stomach.

"Just go. We'll manage. I've changed a few of Gavin's diapers, so I'm sure I can figure things out."

"I'll be in touch." Wade dropped a kiss to Olivia's forehead. "Be a good girl for Peter, Livvie. Daddy and Mommy will be back soon." He swung Rebekah's bag over his shoulder, helped to her feet, and escorted her out the door. The car started then drove away.

There was silence for a few seconds. Peter looked at the toddler. "It's just me and you, baby girl." The two of them and a table full of dirty dishes and leftovers. How was he going to manage all this and a pair of crutches? The orthopedic surgeon had warned him not to put any weight on his right foot for a couple of weeks, and that time was definitely not up yet. Maybe he could employ some child labor carrying items to the dishwasher.

~ ~ ~

"WE'RE ONLY GOING to change one thing this week," said Sierra over the phone on Saturday evening.

Unease swarmed in Sadie's gut. "Oh?"

"I'll be honest here. I don't think I've ever met anyone with a greater aversion to vegetables than you. Looking at the notes from our phone calls this past week, you've had only one full serving, and you hated it."

That about summed it up. "Coleslaw at the diner. It was full of cabbage."

Sierra chuckled. "It usually is. It was probably also drowning in sugar and mayo, but those are topics for another week."

Uh oh. Sadie eyed the tower of caramel espresso pods waiting to be made into decadent brew. She was going to have to give those up, too. She could sense it coming. Her unease plummeted into dread.

"We'll keep up with the daily devotional, the daily walk, and the daily phone call."

Sadie could see where this was going.

"But this week, you're going to make a sincere effort to eat not one, but three full servings of vegetables a day."

"Three?" Sadie gasped. "But..."

"I know it seems like a lot, but I'm going to email you some recipes and tip sheets. You can do this, Sadie."

"I'm not sure I want to."

"Thank you for being honest. How does a life of insulin shots sound to you? Or how about a heart attack? Don't think it can't happen to a woman under the age of thirty. It happens more often than you'd ever guess."

"I looked up some stats."

"Then you know. You made a choice last week, but I'll be honest here. It's not going to be easy to take back your health. These problems didn't crop up overnight, and they're not going to vanish just because you wished upon a star. Changing your trajectory is going to require multiple decisions every single day, but each time you make a choice for positive change, the next one will be a teensy bit easier."

Sadie doubted it. The decision to try again seemed even more difficult after the taste of that lone piece of broccoli and the small bowl of creamy coleslaw.

"How about we start with you packing a lunch to eat at your break?"

"Like... what?"

"A salad. Start with one·cup of torn lettuce. You can chop it yourself or pick up a bag of mixed greens in it if you prefer. I'd like you to pair that with four ounces of protein. A few slices of deli meat, a chicken breast, some salmon, even a boiled egg or two... there are lots of options. And I'd like you to dress that with a low-carb dressing. Since you don't cook or eat vegetables, I'm guessing you don't have any salad dressing in the house."

"You guessed correctly." Sadie braced herself.

"Great! Then there's nothing to stand in the way of a

good choice at the supermarket. Maybe pick up a couple of kinds with carbs below four grams a serving. Don't even worry about how much fat is in them."

Sadie held the phone away from her ear and gave it a quizzical look. "Seriously?"

"Seriously. We'll get into that in a week or two but, for now, just find a dressing you enjoy enough to douse a salad in it every day."

This didn't feel like a baby step. It seemed like a leap into the abyss.

CHAPTER 22

*P*eter thumped into Bridgeview Bakery and Bistro. Wade had dropped him off after work, at his insistence. It was time to start navigating the steep sidewalks again. There was only so long a guy could be a total invalid. He paused, eyes shut, in the doorway, letting the busy place surround him with the mingling aromas of sugar and cinnamon and coffee, the warmth, the gentle hubbub of a gathering place.

"Yo, Santoro!" He turned to find Dan Ranta beckoning him from near the window. Dan had a toddler on his lap with Buddy beside him and Mandy across the table.

Peter motioned to the counter, and Dan nodded. Then Peter hitched himself forward a few steps before his gaze snagged on Sadie. He hadn't seen her, not even at a distance, for over two weeks, which seemed an impossible feat for a next-door neighbor. She stood with her back to him, deep in conversation with Astrid, whose hands gesticulated wildly.

Sadie looked amazing in a swirling knee-length skirt and

a soft-looking top with short, fluttery sleeves. Her blond curls surrounded her head like a halo.

He missed her. Missed being together.

What if he'd gone into a relationship with her more slowly, without that confrontational fight the very first minute? What if he'd acquiesced to her purchase without threatening legal action against her? What if he hadn't had ulterior motives for everything he'd done in the short time they'd dated? Except kissing her the night of the fundraiser. He'd gone into that with blind instinct, and that had also been a mistake. What honorable guy took advantage?

Was he only thinking about her like this because he was lonely? Because he'd watched Wade and Rebekah meld into an even tighter unit since bringing baby Theodore home a few days ago?

No, it wasn't just that. Not at all.

Sadie turned away from Astrid and caught his gaze. Those blue eyes held him fast, and time stood still. She offered an awkward smile — he deserved it — before pivoting and heading to the restroom.

He breathed and completed his journey to the counter, where he ordered two cookies and a cup of black coffee. Kass offered to bring them out for him, so he swung over to Dan's table and lowered himself beside Mandy. He tweaked her nose and grinned when she wrinkled it at him. Then he glanced at Dan. "How're things?"

Dan leaned back in his chair. "Could be better, could be worse."

"Oh? How so? Or is this a bad time to ask?" Peter palmed Mandy's head and tickled her neck.

"No, it's fine. Nothing to hide from the kids. Dixie's

living at her mom's. At least, I think so. She comes down to the house several days a week and stays with the kids while I go to work. Adriana checks in a few times to make sure everything's okay." Dan sighed. "And I drop them off at Fran's if Dixie's not there by seven-thirty."

"Sounds complicated."

"It is." Dan looked past Peter's head and beckoned as Kass set down his order. "Sadie's going to give me some advice."

"I, uh, I should go. I didn't realize you had an appointment."

"It's fine. All of Bridgeview knows my business anyway, and she's your girlfriend, right?"

"Not..." His voice drifted as he caught her vanilla scent.

Kass twisted a chair around from a vacant table and smiled at Sadie before bustling away.

"Really, I don't need to be here." Peter hoisted himself to his feet and reached for his crutches. Then he stared at his cup and plate. Guess he'd just abandon those. Served him right.

"It's fine, Peter. Have a seat." Sadie tucked her skirt under her thighs as she sat. "I was sorry to hear you'd broken your ankle." She set a legal pad on the table and focused on aligning her pen with the edge.

Dan's gaze bounced between them. "Uh..." Yeah, it wouldn't take a genius to figure out they'd hit a snag.

She looked at Dan. "Has anything changed in the past week?"

Dan filled her in, expanding a bit on what he'd told Peter.

Peter's heart ached for his friend as the immensity of

the situation became clear. And still Dan spoke of praying for Dixie's soul as though that were the most vital thing in the world, more important than her relationship with her kids or with him. It was, of course, but Dan's faith had grown in leaps and bounds in the past couple of months, leaving Peter to wonder what had happened to stagnate his own. Was it just that he'd been so busy pushing his own agendas that he'd forgotten to be still before the Lord? Because that had certainly happened.

Sadie made a few notes but agreed that no changes were needed at the moment. Dan should be watchful for signs Dixie's drinking interfered with her ability to parent.

Dan gulped the last of his coffee and pushed back his chair. "I'll see you Monday, then. Come on, kids. Time to go."

Buddy and Mandy followed him out the door, but Peter sat frozen in his seat. Monday? A jealous guy would have wondered if they were dating, but not after the way Dan spoke of Dixie. Plus, there'd been nothing romantic in their conversation, and definitely not in Dan's leave-taking.

Sadie tucked her legal pad into her briefcase and snapped it shut.

"Monday? How often are you meeting with him?"

She glanced at Peter, sucking her lips in for an instant. "Once a week, here, so I can offer counsel in case things change."

"It's Thursday."

She nodded and looked down. "He's coming to start work on the yard Monday."

A steel-toed boot rammed into Peter's mid-section. She was going through with it. But what did it matter? Landon and Jason had dug out all the asparagus one Thursday when Peter was sure she'd be at the office. It was too bad about the raspberries, but it couldn't be helped. He should never have planted perennials on land he didn't own.

He nodded. "I see. Look, I'm sorry. I-I didn't treat you right."

Sadie's chin lifted slightly. "Same. I'm sorry, too. I was flattered by your interest, even though I knew for a fact you were only interested in my backyard. I should have known better." She smoothed her skirt.

"It started that way," he admitted. "But it didn't last long."

"I understand. No one could be interested in me, not with all this extra weight and—"

"Is that what you think? Because that's not what happened."

She blinked, her glance bouncing off his for an instant. "But..."

"But then I started to fall for you, for real, and I knew I'd started off all wrong and didn't know how to rebuild on the right footing."

"You... fell for me?"

Peter leaned closer. "I did, but I couldn't separate my feelings for you from my anxiety about the yard. You know what I realized?"

She shook her head, a look of wonder in her blue eyes.

"I realized what I should have known all along. That I was treating Mrs. Essery's property — now yours — as though I owned it. Instead of taking a big step back, and hearing your words, and praying about the situation, and getting to know you for *you*, I leaped in with both feet and my mouth flapping. And then... how could I retract all that? I didn't know how. I'm sorry."

SADIE TWISTED her hands together in her lap. Could Peter be telling the truth? But there was no reason for him to lie. A furtive glance his direction revealed his focus on her, his blue eyes filled with vulnerability, regret, and maybe hope, but not with sympathy or revulsion. He was waiting for her to say something. To respond. But, how could she?

The hubbub of the bistro surrounded them with people talking and laughing and the coffee machine grinding. Sugar in unending, tantalizing forms danced in the warm, humid atmosphere.

She was going to remember this moment forever, no matter what happened next. And what happened next depended a great deal on her response. How much she wanted to be loved paled in comparison to how much she needed to grow in her faith and tackle her own health. But, oh, how she wanted to be loved. Romanced. Not just by any man, but by this one. Despite all that had happened, he'd wrapped around her heart and hadn't let go.

"Peter. I..." Words failed her, and she bit her lip.

His gaze dropped to her mouth for a brief instant before focusing again on her eyes. Just that little hint of masculine desire gave her courage.

"You have nothing to be sorry for, Peter. It was all me. My insecurities. My... issues. I sent such mixed signals, from courtroom lawyer to... well, the opposite. I'm really not good at relationships. I'd like to blame my parents, but it's time I took responsibility. I'm a grownup — I spent seven years in college, studied all aspects of law, and passed the bar exams. But all this time, I've been hiding."

His hand covered hers on her lap. The warm clasp brought tears to her eyes, but she blinked them back as she turned her hand over and laced her fingers with his.

"I'm unhealthy, Peter. I'm having some health issues because I'm fat."

He opened his mouth as though to protest, but she shook her head.

"I am. Somehow I've always been able to dodge accepting responsibility. I blamed my unknown genetics. I blamed my hectic schedule. I blamed everything but myself." She took a deep breath. "My doctor laid it out for me. How I'm at extreme risk for diabetes. Heart disease. Even cancer. Sure, all those things can happen to thin people, too, but the risk is much greater for those who are, um... obese."

Even in this moment of honesty, she couldn't quite make herself say the adjective. *Morbidly* obese.

"Sadie, you have so much courage. I'm in awe."

"Courage?" She blinked at him. "I'm not sure that's the right word at all. It's like I woke up in a hall of mirrors, with the truth jabbing its fingers at me from all sides until I couldn't pretend anymore."

His fingers squeezed hers and, oh, his lopsided grin gave her some of that courage he spoke of.

"I'm done with that now. I take responsibility. It's not going to be easy..." Oh, man. Wasn't that the understatement of the decade? "Denae helped me find a coach, a

Christian woman who's in touch daily and who's walking through this with me."

"That's amazing. *You're* amazing."

"You don't need to flatter me."

Peter shook his head, but the warmth in his smile didn't falter. "No flattery. Only honesty. I'm really impressed at how you're facing this head-on, but I shouldn't be surprised. It's one of the things I like best about you, after all. Your directness. Your focus. Your ability to get things done."

She opened her mouth and closed it again. It was as though the act ushered in warmth and peace that trickled into her every cell. Was that really how he saw her? He believed in her?

"You mentioned a coach." Peter looked down at their clasped hands as his thumb smoothed circles on the side of hers, sending tingles up her arm. "Is she someone local? How is that going?"

"There's a place in northern Idaho called Green Acres Farm. I've gone up there the past two weekends—"

His face lit up. "You're kidding. Green Acres? They do amazing stuff. I've gone to a few workshops they've hosted in the past couple of years, and so has Jasmine. In fact, one of my friends — have you met Jacob and Eden? They live down by the river. Eden works for Animal Control and Jacob is a solar architect. Anyway, Jacob's two sisters live at Green Acres."

She should have known Peter would be familiar with the place and the people. The whole atmosphere at the farm had reminded her of Bridgeview with friends and neighbors forming a true community. "I don't think I've met them, but

Sierra mentioned her brother living here. That's who I'm working with. Sierra Rubachuk. She's had some weight and health struggles." Sadie took a deep breath. "Not quite like mine, but enough that she's worked hard to find solutions."

Peter nodded slowly, his gaze intent on hers. "What are you doing together? If you don't mind my asking."

Did she mind? Not even a little. For the first time in... well, forever, she felt like someone was at her side, honestly caring about her and guiding her in all truth. Sure, Denae was her good friend, but she seemed to have enough eating issues of her own, albeit the opposite kind. But with Sierra and the rest of the Green Acres team — and now, maybe, Peter? — the mountain looked climbable.

"She's created a plan. The first thing is that she sends me a devotional every morning by email. They contain scripture verses and meditations about God's love for me and about my response to Him. I guess they're more about my mental and spiritual health than about my physical health."

"Sounds like a great foundation, though. The best."

Sadie nodded. "It's super helpful. Then I'm supposed to walk for half an hour every day. I've been doing that at lunchtime, around the block by the office. It's a whole lot flatter downtown than in Bridgeview."

He tossed back his head and laughed. Man, he looked good. His dark hair slightly tousled, his face tanned from working outside and creased with laugh lines, his teeth even and white in the midst of his trim beard. "It is that," he said, still chuckling.

"And the third thing is the hardest, so far. Vegetables."

The grin hadn't wiped off his face. "Veggies are awesome. So many kinds, so many ways to fix them."

"I'm trying to get up to three servings a day." She wrinkled her nose. "Sierra says we're shooting for more like ten by the end of this, but, wow, I'm not sure I can do it."

"Salads. Stir-fries. Stews."

"You have an answer for everything."

Peter's eyes sobered slightly as they searched her face. "I'm the guy who messed everything up. I have no answers."

"But you like veggies."

"Well, yeah." He shrugged. "That doesn't make me a saint or anything."

She'd let that go for the moment. "Sierra also said I'm going to be giving up sugar and other empty carbs in a week or two." Full-bore panic threatened to overwhelm her every time she let the thought poke into her head.

His eyes widened. "I love my veggies, but I'm not sure I could survive without sugar."

"That's what I said. Not the part about vegetables. But then I got to thinking about how..." She took a deep breath. "How Astrid harps on the evils of sugar and that there are other sweeteners that are better for you. That's what we were talking about a few minutes ago. She's going to bake me some cookies she said will meet all of Sierra's guidelines."

"That's awesome. I admit I don't really know anything about that."

"I'm soon going to know more than I ever dreamed of. I'm not going to lie. It's going to be a ginormous challenge."

"But you're going to do it?" Admiration tinged his question.

Sadie lifted her chin just a smidge. "I *so* am. Sierra tells me baby steps are okay. That it took more than a week or two to get me into this mess, and it will take more than a week or two to get out of it. She also says I'm going to make mistakes, and we're just going to keep going. She's introducing me to a program called Trim Healthy Mama, and we're easing into it slowly."

"I didn't know how much I liked Jacob's sister." Peter leaned a little closer across the corner of the table. "But not as much as I like you. Can I... might there be a little corner of your life where I might fit? I've missed you."

"There might be." Her heart sang in wonder. "I've missed you, too."

CHAPTER 23

"*A*w, I knew Mr. Gorgeous really cared beneath all that other stuff."

Sadie shook her head, grinning at her friend's sultry tone. She stood in her backyard, secure in the knowledge that no one was home next door to overhear her conversation. She'd watched them all leave over an hour ago, Peter in his truck with Jasmine driving and the back loaded with vegetables for the downtown market.

"I'm scared I'm going to sabotage everything." Again.

"I'm sure you'll mess up."

"Great. Thanks."

"No, I mean it. He's going to blow it again, too. I can promise you that."

"Is that what you've learned from editing hundreds of romance novels? Everyone keeps screwing up?" Made sense. Denae's comments about the stories she worked on had shown Sadie the rhythm of fiction, but that was only because it *was* fiction, right? Stories needed conflict, or they'd be boring to read, but real life shouldn't run on drama.

"No, it's what I've learned from observing human nature."

Drat. Not what Sadie wanted to hear at all. "Oh?"

"Want to know the single most important phrase in a marriage?"

"I love you?" Because Peter was going to say those words any day now. She could feel them coming.

"Uh uh. 'I was wrong. I'm sorry.' Because human nature will show through, and you will act selfishly... and so will he. Admitting it when you blow it and eating humble pie will make all the difference."

That made altogether too much sense. "I pity the guy you'll eventually marry."

Denae chuckled. "Why's that?"

"Because you're going to psychoanalyze him to death. What guy will want to be presented with a checklist of the stages of relationship and what's appropriate for each one?"

"I wouldn't do that!"

"You will so. At least in your head, and I bet you'll let the words slip at some point and scare the poor guy into running."

There was a moment of silence. "Do you really think that I'll scare him away?" Denae's voice had lost its usual vibrancy.

Sadie caved. "Not if you're careful to keep all your knowledge zipped inside."

"I see what you mean. I promise I'll be careful. That is, if I ever meet a man who's even attracted to me at all."

"How could they not be? You're gorgeous. You're skinny. You're—"

"Messed up."

"Now wait a minute, missy. You are not messed up. You're the best friend a girl could ever wish for."

"Thanks. I put on a good front, I guess. Just like you did for all these years, pretending you were happy and fulfilled and all that."

Sadie paced across the lush grass in her backyard. If Ranta Landscaping weren't digging things out on Monday, this would definitely need mowing. "I didn't think I convinced anyone."

"Sure you did." Denae scoffed. "Ms. Self-Sufficient Attorney at her finest. You didn't need anyone."

"Except my mother."

"Well, yeah. But you didn't let most people know about that. Instead, you went into family law, so you could help other adoptive and foster kids as much as you could. You can say whatever you like, Sadie, but you've made a real difference in a lot of people's lives. In mine."

"Really? I thought you only put up with me because we were kids together in Cannon Beach."

"No way. I mean, that's how it started, but I haven't kept up with Karen or Macy or the other girls in our class. Have you?"

"No. Not since grad." Was it true that Denae wasn't just putting up with her from some sense of guilt? Something lightened inside Sadie and put a spring in her step.

She peered at the raspberry canes and noticed a few deep red berries amid the lighter ones and flowers. Were those ripe? She pulled on one, and it came off easily in her hand, leaving a tiny cone behind. Was that normal? She popped the berry in her mouth and couldn't help the smile as the sweetness exploded.

Maybe this diet wouldn't be so bad. Oh, wait. Sierra refused to call Trim Healthy Mama a diet. She said diet was a word with negative connotations when, in reality, it only meant way of eating. Okay, so Sadie's new way of eating included berries, and this one had been delish. She hunted for another.

"Sadie?"

"Hmm?" She reached into the thicket of prickly canes and green leaves for another berry.

"What are you doing?"

"Just discovered my raspberries have fruit on them, and they're actually very tasty."

Denae whooped into the phone, and Sadie pulled the device from her ear until her friend subsided.

"But there's something else." Sadie narrowed her gaze at a row of green leaves at the base of the canes. Each leafy tuft seemed to grow from a partially submerged red ball. Radishes? She cringed as she remembered the day she'd caught Jasmine planting them, but hadn't the teens removed the radishes along with the asparagus? Maybe they'd missed this row tucked against the berry patch.

She leaned down and pulled a plant. That red globe, about an inch across, had to be a radish. It was a vegetable, right? One in high demand for Bridgeview Backyards. "Denae? Have you ever eaten a radish?"

Her friend snickered. "Only like a thousand times."

"There's one in my hand." She brushed off the dirt clinging to the root. "I'm going to take a bite."

"It's pep—"

Sadie bit down. Whoa! She spat it out, but the taste lingered. "That's horrid!"

"I told you. There's a reason they slice them super thin for salads. Or cook them."

Cook them? Wait, what had Jasmine talked about that day? A life lesson. That radishes were hard and bitter when raw, but soft and mild when cooked. Well, she'd been right about the raw flavor, for sure. The little balls must be the primary ingredient in pepper spray.

Sadie yanked out two more of the little globes. "How do I cook them?"

"Um... are you serious?"

"I'm going to do this, by golly, and I'm going to like it." Her tongue still tingled with the fire of one small bite. "I need a drink to cut the spice first, though."

"Go you! I'm impressed. Is this Sierra's doing? Because I totally owe the woman one if it is."

"Partly, and partly Peter. They sell a lot of radishes. Someone even placed a special order for tons of them, which is how there are plants growing in my yard." Sadie marched toward the door. "Tell me what to do with them."

"Cut the leaves and the root end off and wash them."

Sadie dumped them in the sink and set the phone on speaker on the window ledge before grabbing a knife. "Are the leaves edible?"

"They are. Sadie, are you okay? Because this isn't like you."

"I told you. I'm a new woman, and I'm going to be half the woman I am today. And I might need to like radishes to get there." She turned on the tap.

"Wow, okay. Depending on the radish, the leaves might have a weird hairy texture. Those are better cooked, but if they're smooth, you can eat them raw or cooked. Add them chopped up into a salad."

Sadie rubbed a leaf. Didn't feel hairy to her, so she took a bite. "Meh, not that good."

Denae giggled. "I like this new, adventurous friend. Soon you'll be teaching me a thing or two about vegetables."

"Wow, LOOK AT ALL THIS PRODUCE." A woman ran her hand along the edge of the row of baskets that lined the front of the market table. "No peas today? I bought some last week and they were so tender and sweet."

Peter stood behind the table, braced on his crutches. "I'm sorry. The crop is slowing down, and all the peas went into the subscription boxes this week. Same with the raspberries, though that crop is just starting. We only bring the extras to the market."

He'd noticed the raspberries ripening through the fence that divided Alex's yard from Sadie's, but they weren't his for the picking. He needed to talk to her about them, though. Maybe with her new diet, she'd be willing to keep them for her own use rather than have Dan dig up the canes.

The woman grinned. "Then I guess we'd better sign up for a subscription, if you still have some available."

"We sure do." Peter shuffled to one side, picked up a brochure from the rack, and handed it to her. "My cousin and I are still in the process of establishing our business, but we can take on two or three more regular customers this year. We'll need more yards for next season if we're to grow our subscriber base any further."

The woman scanned the paper then glanced up. "You're based in Bridgeview? We live just up the hill from there. What kind of yards are you looking for?"

Peter chuckled. "Large and flat, preferably. We can put in raised beds or work directly in the soil, depending on the situation. We're currently asking homeowners to sign five-year agreements."

"That makes sense. I imagine you put a lot of work into building up the garden, so you wouldn't want that to go to waste."

Peter hid the grimace that accompanied the reminder. "Exactly right. We had one property sold from under us this year, and that put us in a bit of a bind... but it happens."

"My name is Irene Smith." She extended her hand across the table.

He shook it. "Peter Santoro."

"I'll talk to my husband about it, but we're both so busy we're doing nothing with our space. His elderly parents live next door, plus they have a vacant lot on the other side. They've been hiring a lawn care company the past few years."

It sounded too good to be true. "Not only do we not charge for caring for the yard, we offer incentives, such as a discount on the subscription boxes."

Irene beamed. "Win, win." She fluttered the paper. "I'll be in touch later today. There might be a few other neighbors who'd want in on it. How many more yards do you need?"

Peter's brain reeled. If they signed several more spaces, he'd be able to resign from Fish and Wildlife... at least if they could increase the subscriptions at the same rate. He and Jasmine might still need to hire a seasonal worker or two. Growth was good, but how much was too much? How quickly was too quickly? They'd suffered some severe setbacks already since starting the business what with having to buy out Basil and then Sadie's purchase of Mrs. Essery's house. Everything was such a gamble.

Peace I leave with you; my peace I give you... do not be afraid.

From John chapter fourteen, wasn't it? He and Jasmine had done a lot of praying over the business, especially in the past few weeks. Was this an answer?

They'd be a bit more cautious now, but they still needed to grow. "My phone number's on the back. My business partner and I would be happy to swing by later to see the spaces and answer any questions you might have."

"That sounds great. Fresh veggies *and* less yard work. What could be better?"

Peter grinned. "I totally agree."

He added up Irene's purchase of broccoli, beans, and herbs, ignoring the sound of his buzzing phone. When she'd walked away, promising to call later, he snatched up his cell.

Basil's name appeared on his screen along with *missed call*.

Basil? No one had heard from him in a while.

"Oh, look, honey. They have beets!"

Peter pocketed his phone and turned to the new customers. He'd have to call his cousin back later. The time didn't come until the market closed two hours later and Landon returned to load up the remains. It killed Peter not to help, but there wasn't much he could do with his hands tied up with the crutches.

He stepped aside to tap Basil's number. "Hey, sorry I missed your call. I was in the middle of the downtown market. What's up, man?"

"You and Jasmine still doing that?"

No thanks to Basil. "Yep, sure are. Landon and Jason — you know, Nathan's brother — are working for us this summer. I broke my ankle just before Hoopfest—"

"Heard about that from Dominic."

Peter's ears perked up. He hadn't known the two guys ever ran into each other in Seattle. Basil was seven years older than Dom. It wasn't like they had much in common with each other. "Oh, yeah?"

"He looked me up when he got back to the Emerald City."

"Spoken like a true Seattleite." Peter kept his tone light.

"The place grows on a guy."

Until that moment, Peter hadn't realized how much he'd expected his cousin to move back to Spokane. Hoped for it. "Sorry to hear that. I miss having you around."

"Sure, you do."

"Definitely."

Basil laughed. "It's okay, man. You don't have to lie. I know I screwed up and everyone's lives are much more peaceful without me around."

"Is that what you think? Because that's not reality, not even a little bit. Nonna asks every week if someone has heard from you. The aunts all ask each other for scraps of news then ask our generation. Everyone is praying for you, Basil. We miss you, and we wish you'd come home."

"Nice sentiment, but I don't think so. There's too much pressure on a Santoro in Bridgeview. You've got to know what I mean."

"Dude? I think you're mistaking Nonna for God."

Basil's sharp laugh came through the phone. "Nonna's not God. I'm perfectly aware of that."

"That's not exactly what I meant. I meant...you think you're running from Nonna's displeasure, but you're really running from God. And you can't. Have a look at Psalm 139, Basil. 'Where can I go from your Spirit? Where can I flee from your presence? If I go up to the heavens, you are there; if I make my bed in the depths, you are there. If I rise on the wings of the dawn, if I settle on the far side of the sea, even there your hand will guide me, your right hand will hold me fast.'"

"Look at you, all quoting scripture like a good Sunday School boy."

Was there a hint of longing in the sardonic words? "Psalm 139, Basil. Landon's here to help me pack up the market, so I've got to go. Call me again sometime. Don't be a stranger."

CHAPTER 24

I'll send Jason and Landon in to dig out the raspberry canes." Peter winced as he realized he should have done that sooner, but the crop had just begun.

Sadie sat on her back step beside him. "I don't know anything about how they grow, but you can leave them. They're not taking up much space along that edge."

He angled her way. "But you wanted to put a water feature there." Work had started on the space. Dan had been in with his little Bobcat and removed the patch of lawn and the tiny decrepit patio with its uneven, broken concrete. Over the past week, he'd prepared a frost-resistant base for the new red-brick patio.

Huh. He and Sadie had started off all wrong the first time, too, without a proper foundation. No wonder their relationship had broken when they'd done the same as dumping concrete on top of grass and expecting it to stay level and strong. Not this time. Now they were building a real foundation. Sadie shared her morning emails from Sierra with him. They read scripture and prayed together, and he tried to support every baby step she made on the health and veggie front.

But this? While part of him hoped they had a future together that would mean this yard would one day be their oasis, not just hers, he didn't want to head down that slippery slope of possessiveness any time soon. "Don't change your plans for me, honey. Just don't."

She leaned against his shoulder. "It's not just that. Sierra said raspberries are one of the best fruits since they're low-glycemic and packed with vitamins and stuff. So, I've been picking a few of them. They're not half bad."

Low-glycemic hadn't been in his vocabulary before embarking on this journey with Sadie, but he'd learned a lot in the past few weeks. He wouldn't have believed it possible to see such a difference in a person. Even before she told him she'd lost fifteen pounds, he could see the difference on her, but it was more than the fit of her clothes. She could walk as quickly as he and his crutches could. And she glowed.

"My nonna makes a lot of desserts with raspberries." As soon as the words left Peter's mouth, he could have kicked himself. It was true, of course, but the recipes were full of sugar and white flour and butter and probably other ingredients on Sadie's no-go list. "They're my favorite berries," he finished lamely.

"Astrid brought me some raspberry cheesecake brownies yesterday."

Peter blinked at Sadie. "She what?"

"It's amazing! And the recipe met Sierra's approval."

He gave his head a shake. "I never know when you're pulling my leg and when you're serious."

"I'm serious. Want a taste?" She braced her hands on the step and pushed herself to standing.

"I... uh, sure. Why not?" He knew why not. Of course, sugar was bad if a person went overboard — and Sadie had — but replacements had to be an evil of their own. Personally, he'd go straight to honey, but apparently that was too high-glycemic for constant use, too. A guy couldn't win, so his best bet was to eat his veggies and stay active, so he could indulge whenever he wanted.

Peter could hear Sadie clanking around in the kitchen and only hoped he could fake enthusiasm well enough to encourage her. His gaze roved the backyard, already so changed from Mrs. Essery's day. Was he doing the right thing, dating Sadie, or did the whole garden thing still keep things awkward?

No. He liked her. A lot. Those weeks where they'd been at odds had been long and painful. He might even be falling in love with her. That meant he needed to be honest about the dessert she was bringing for him. There was no room for fake. Not anymore. Not ever.

"I nearly forgot she brought me some raspberry soda, too." She handed him a glass from the tray she set on the landing.

He eyed it. The red liquid over ice cubes looked normal enough, but he dreaded the first sip. He wasn't getting away without trying it, though, not with her anxious gaze pinned on his.

Lord? You turned water into wine, so can You turn this sugar-free beverage into something tasty? Sadie needs the encouragement as much as the wedding-goers in Cana did.

Peter lifted the glass to his lips, steeled his expression,

and took a sip. A mix of sweet and tart and refreshing chill rolled over his tongue. He opened his eyes and looked at the glass again before taking a second sip. "Th-that's actually not too bad." *Thank You, God, for answering my prayer.*

Sadie grinned, even her eyes smiling. "It's not exactly a cream soda, but I quite like it." She gestured toward the berry patch. "According to Astrid and Sierra, I need to pick and freeze all the ripe berries." Then her face fell. "But you've got customers waiting for them."

He shook his head. "They're yours, and freezing them is a good idea. A client of Nathan's offered us an established berry patch in Airway Heights. It's outside of Bridgeview so not ideal, but it will tide us over."

"Are you sure?" She watched him over the rim of her glass.

"Absolutely." He leaned closer and touched his lips to hers. Wow, that electricity wasn't getting old anytime soon. "Your health and happiness is the most important thing to me."

Those blue eyes searched his face. "That's the sweetest thing anyone has ever said to me."

"*You're* the sweetest thing that ever happened to me." He set the glass behind him and gathered her close, kissing her more thoroughly. Yes, he was definitely falling in love with this woman.

Sadie pulled away a moment later. "You haven't tried the cheesecake brownies yet."

"I'm not really hungry?" Not for sugar-free sweets, anyway.

She lifted a plate and forked a bite off the gooey brownie marbled with a white filling. One of several raspberries rolled off the fork as she pointed it toward his mouth.

Peter knew when he'd lost the battle, so he opened his mouth and accepted the bite. The rich chocolate caressed his tongue and the cream cheese mellowed the slight after-taste while the raspberries popped with a refreshing burst.

"That's... nice." But he needed to say what he was think-ing. "The only thing is, I'm worried about the chemicals in the sweeteners. Aren't they as bad for you as sugar, or even worse? I've heard so many horror stories about chemical sweeteners like aspartame."

"I've heard those, too. Honestly, I used those stories to avoid thinking too much about my habits. Astrid intro-duced me to natural sweeteners like stevia and some plant-based blends." Sadie wrinkled her nose. "Some of them don't taste very good, but Astrid says that if I stay off sugar, my taste buds will adjust and the aftertaste will go away. Did you taste something odd?"

"Well... a little bit. Not as much as I expected."

She laughed. "I could tell you were dreading it." Her face sobered. "I'm not going to lie. Cutting out sugar has been brutal. I've been totally addicted to the stuff all my life. It means a lot that you're supporting me in this. Between Sierra and Astrid, they're supplying me with all kinds of resources, but... they're not you. They're not part of my life. Not really."

"Sadie?"

She peeked up at him through long lashes.

"I'm not going anywhere. I think I'm falling in love with you." He cradled her face between his hands as he swept a gentle kiss over her lips. "I hope you feel the same."

SADIE'S HEART sang at his sweet words. She didn't deserve this man. He was kind and thoughtful and encouraging. It was a fine line. She knew that, but he said all the right things. His words, his caring, washed away her ugly realities like a gentle summer rain refreshing the earth and softening hard ridges.

She leaned against his shoulder as they sat on the steps, his arm snug around her back, his fingers caressing her waist. And, when he pressed a kiss into her curls, Sadie knew beyond a shadow of a doubt that Peter Santoro was the real thing. Authentic. Those raindrops of his approval had soaked into her shriveled heart and she did, in fact, know how to love someone back.

Peter. She loved Peter.

This moment would be etched in her memory forever. The back step shaded with that huge maple, but the air warm and still. A few bees buzzed — she knew now that they came from the hives Jasmine had tucked in the far corner of the house next door. The fragrance of Mrs. Essery's heirloom roses on either side of the steps mingled with the chocolate and raspberry aromas beside Sadie. There could never be a more perfect moment than this.

"Sadie?"

Her eyes sprang open at Stan's voice, and she pulled away from Peter. Not that he let her go until she surged to her feet. "Stan?"

But someone followed Stan around the corner of the house. A middle-aged woman she didn't know yet who looked strangely familiar. With a jolt, Sadie recognized herself in fifteen or twenty years.

She swayed, but Peter had clambered to his feet, cast and all, and caught her arm. Grounded her. Sadie took a sharp breath, unable to stop staring.

"Hi, Stan." Peter's voice. Peter's arm around her waist. Peter's support surrounding her.

Sadie blinked and looked at her adoptive father. "What's going on?"

He looked a great deal older than his sixty-five years. "I brought someone to meet you."

"I see that." And who this person was seemed obvious, but how did Stan know? What was the connection?

"Sadie, I want you to meet Lynda's cousin Jackie. You probably don't remember her — you haven't seen her since you were a preschooler. Jackie is..." He closed his eyes for a moment, his face ashen. "Jackie is the woman who gave birth to you."

Sadie's gaze riveted on Jackie's face. Her mother. The one who'd given her away as a newborn. The one she'd never heard from since. Was it Jackie's fault, or had Stan and Lynda insisted? Why had they made this decision then stuck to it when records opened up most places? Questions tumbled over each other in her mind, each trying to be the first to explode out of her mouth.

"I'm glad you're here, Jackie," said Peter, his arm steady against her back. "I'm Peter Santoro, Sadie's boyfriend. I know she's wanted to meet you for a long time."

Peter to the rescue. All those other things didn't matter. The anger and frustration with Stan didn't matter. Jackie was here. Her mother.

Sadie found her voice. "As you can see, my backyard is under construction." She waved a trembling hand. "Why don't you come inside? We can have a seat and talk about this."

Stan nodded, his gaze shifting between her and Peter. "That might be a good idea. I'm sorry for springing this on you, but your words of needing to know your medical history pushed me to open this door, and Jackie flew right out when I phoned her. I should have warned you."

The worry would have given her ulcers. "It's fine." She tightened her fingers around Peter's and peeked up at him. "You have a few more minutes, don't you?"

"Absolutely."

Peter the rock, just like the biblical disciple. She could depend on this man no matter what happened in the next few minutes. Sadie led the way into the house then allowed Peter to take her guests through to the living room while she assembled a tray of raspberry sodas, using all the concentrate Astrid had given her. She'd need the recipe to make more. She braced her hands on the kitchen counter and looked out the window, the voices from the other room a backdrop she could ignore for a brief moment.

"Lord, please keep my words gracious and kind," she whispered. "I'm so overwhelmed." She took a deep breath. If she could detach her emotions in a court case, she could do this... only it was her own life. Yet, Jesus could give her peace. "Thank You."

She picked up the tray and headed for the living room, holding out the tray first to Jackie, who sat on the edge of the sofa. Sadie managed a smile. Her mother.

"I was fourteen," Jackie blurted. "I didn't know what to

do. Certainly, I was too young to marry the boy — your father." She winced. "I waited as long as possible to tell my parents. They were horrified that I'd been such a rebellious child and devised a plan quicker than I could blink. My mom's cousin Lynda was much younger than her, married, and unable to conceive. I was sent to stay with them in Naperville until the baby was born." Tears gushed down the woman's face. "You."

Sadie set the tray on the coffee table and knelt awkwardly in front of Jackie, clutching her twisting hands in her own. A month ago, she'd never have made it down... at least with any hope of getting upright again afterward. Now, it was the least of her worries. She tried to put herself in the pregnant teen's situation and realized Peter's sister had been right there. What a difference a supportive family made. She swallowed the lump in her throat.

"I signed the papers right after your birth with my parents looming over my shoulder." Jackie's voice broke. "I never got to hold you or even see you. Everyone said it was better that way. We were on the next flight back to Marion, and I started my tenth-grade year two weeks late. No one at home knew."

Sadie could think of no words. Tears dribbled down her cheeks.

"We moved to Oregon a few months later," Stan said, sadness in his voice. "Jackie's parents returned our Christmas cards unopened, proving they meant it when they'd asked for no contact. We didn't quite realize we'd never be welcome in the family again, but we didn't regret our choice to adopt you. Lynda loved you like her own, Sadie. So did I. I'm just lousy at showing it."

Peter cleared his throat. "I understand a little of what you went through, Jackie. My teenage sister's little guy just turned one. When Dafne found out she was pregnant, she ran away with her boyfriend to abort, but she couldn't do it. Everything was really messy when she came home a few weeks later. She and my parents had a lot to work through as they tried to find solutions that would work. I witnessed the hormone-fueled words — both Dafne's and our mom's. Just saying... I get it."

Anger tried to resurge in Sadie's chest, but it washed away at Peter's words. Anger would only set healing back. And what she wanted most were healthy, honest relationships.

Sadie shifted on her knees and squeezed Jackie's hands until the woman met her gaze through red-rimmed eyes. "I forgive you." It felt good. Freeing. Like she could float into the sky. She struggled to her feet and turned to Stan. Really looked at him. After all this time, how could she even begin to make amends?

Was that a tear or two snaking down his face as he rose to meet her? "Sadie, I know I haven't been everything you needed but, despite everything, your mom and I were so happy to be your parents. We were so thankful for you. I still am."

She let him hold her then and, for the first time in forever, she hugged him back. "I'm sorry, Stan. I've been so selfish, seeing everything as all about me and forgetting that others had valid feelings, too. Can you forgive me?"

"Absolutely. But, I need forgiveness, too. I didn't know how to be a father and, instead of just jumping in, hanging out with you, and doing my best, I convinced myself that providing you with all the gadgets and things was my best bet. I worked too many hours when I should have been focusing on you. I'm sorry, honey."

"I forgive you." Freedom and lightness filled Sadie's heart. "You only live twenty minutes away now. We have the rest of our lives to build that relationship, if you want to. Dad." Man, she hadn't called him that in years.

Those were definitely tears. They mingled with the ones she shed as he held her close. "Thank you. You have no idea what that means to me."

*A*re you still cold?" Peter set a lid on the cast iron frying pan and turned from the stove when Sadie padded into her kitchen wearing thick sweats and fuzzy socks, arms wrapped around herself.

She nestled against his side, and he drew her in with his free arm. He flipped the burner off. Never mind what he'd been doing. Supper could wait, though it was already late since they'd volunteered at Blessings Under the Bridge after work.

He pressed a kiss against her blond curls, still damp from her shower, as he gathered her close.

"A little," she admitted. "I have an entire new appreciation for everything God has given me, though. A cozy home and good food to eat, for starters." She leaned around him to peer at the frying pan. "What have you got there, anyway?"

Peter turned her away from the stove. "Not telling."

She laughed as she looked up at him. "While I'm on the

thanksgiving train, I'm also thankful for a boyfriend who can cook. It smells amazing."

He covered her mouth with his, savoring the taste of her, the vanilla scent of her shampoo, the warmth of her in his arms. "I'm thankful for you," he murmured at last. "Your compassion." He kissed her. "Your beauty." Another kiss. "Your focus and strength."

The timer buzzed from behind him. He kissed her again then gave her a nudge. "Pour a couple of glasses of that soda you've been hiding and go have a seat in the dining room. I'll plate up and be right with you."

"I can help." Sadie batted her eyelashes at him. "I haven't burned anything in over a week."

Peter grinned. It was true that she'd come a long way in the past four months. She'd driven to Green Acres Farm a couple of weekends a month and was flourishing under Sierra's mentorship and friendship. Still, it was entirely possible cooking would never be her thing. For himself, he'd learned he quite enjoyed it when he had someone as appreciative as Sadie to cook for. She was also more adventuresome than he'd ever have guessed.

Ice clanked as she pressed a glass to the fridge dispenser. He gave his head a shake and removed the frying pan lid then sprinkled seasoning and freshly grated parmesan over the scallops. When Sadie left the room, he pulled the roasted veggies out of the oven, turned the dial to broil, and tucked the scallops inside.

A few weeks ago, Stan had given Lynda's china to Sadie, and they'd displayed it in Mrs. Essery's china cabinet. Peter arranged roasted asparagus and radishes on two plates then added the scallops beside them. Now for the balsamic reduction, which he dribbled in a spiral over the food. *Thank you, Food Network, for keeping me and my broken ankle company last summer.*

"This looks and smells amazing." Sadie's eyes grew wide as he set her plate in front of her. "What did I do to deserve you in my life?"

He gave her a quick kiss then took his seat around the corner. "I could ask the same, but I suspect the answer is that God doesn't give us what we deserve. He just loves us." Peter reached for Sadie's hand. "May I ask the blessing?"

After grace, they began to eat.

"Where did you find asparagus this time of year?" Sadie asked, spearing a piece with her fork.

He grinned. "Safeway. As we head into Thanksgiving, I had to give a nod to how far we've come in the past eight months, and asparagus and radishes are part of our story."

"I never thought I'd like either of them."

"I know. This particular recipe was shared by one of our market regulars. Alex and I made it a bunch of times back in May and June."

"It's delicious." Sadie gave him a small smile. "I can't believe all the things I've learned to like, from radishes to kale chips." She swept her hands down her sides. "And who knew a person didn't need to do anything extreme to lose weight. Besides cutting out sugar and learning to eat veggies. It's funny, but those things don't seem extreme anymore."

Peter captured her hand. She'd told him it was forty pounds gone, but those numbers weren't his focus. He saw the spring in her step, the glow on her face, and the sparkle in her eyes. She was so much healthier than she'd been.

Maybe when spring came around, he'd teach her to shoot hoops. "You saw your doctor this morning?"

"I did. All those nasty numbers are coming into range. The blood pressure, the cholesterol, the blood glucose...everything. She's really pleased. She also reminded me that weight loss will likely slow down now, after the first big drop. And that not everyone will have the same success I've had."

"I'm so proud of you. You've worked hard for that."

Sadie beamed. "I think God knew I needed the encouragement. Hey, I've got one more trip to Green Acres planned this fall — first weekend in December. Would you come, too? I'd like you to meet everyone. Sierra said there are plenty of guest rooms."

"I'd love to." Finally, finally, the market season was over. Jasmine had delivered the last subscription boxes earlier today. There'd be some much-needed downtime over the winter while they analyzed this year's growth and determined future plans.

Peter pushed back his chair. "Ready for dessert?"

"I'm not sure I can eat another bite."

Wrong answer. "Aw, come on. I had Astrid bake something special for you. Pumpkin cheesecake. Try a few bites?"

No guilt pushing sweets at her. Astrid was totally on board with all the Trim Healthy Mama guidelines Sierra had laid out for Sadie. The name had made Peter wince until Sadie had laughingly told him a lot of families did it together. Some guys even called it the Man Plan.

"You twisted my arm." She started to rise, but he shook his head. "Today's my day to serve you."

Peter carried the plates into the kitchen, pulled the

container of cheesecake out of the fridge, and plated two pieces before adding a dollop of whipped cream to each. He took a deep breath, patted his pocket, and sent a quick prayer heavenward before returning to the dining room.

"That looks amazing. Astrid works miracles." Sadie lifted her fork. "I'm so glad I didn't have to starve myself for these results. Or drink chemical-laden shakes."

"Kass and Hailey are even going to introduce several sugar-free desserts to the bakery menu in the new year." Peter took his own seat. "Turns out there's more demand than they ever dreamed existed, so it might be a new niche for them. Nathan's working on a marketing plan with them to launch the new line." Why was he babbling on about things that didn't matter? He didn't usually stall. Didn't usually have any trouble speaking his mind. He cleared his throat. "Sadie?"

She paused, loaded fork halfway to her mouth. "Yes?"

Bad timing. He needed to wait until dinner was over. "You're beautiful."

Sadie gave him a puzzled smile. "Thank you."

A few minutes later, she rose and folded her napkin. "Peter, I can't thank you enough. This was an amazing pre-Thanksgiving dinner. It was so thoughtful of you, knowing how crazy busy things will be tomorrow with your family get-together."

He stood and gathered her in his arms. "I've got something I want to ask you."

Sadie stretched to plant a kiss on his mouth. "The answer is yes."

"You don't even know what the question is."

"I don't need to."

Peter took a deep breath. "I think you do, because it's a pretty big one." He dug the little box out of his pocket and dropped to one knee. "Will you marry me? I love you so much, and I can't imagine life without you." He put his heart in his eyes as he looked up at her.

"Oh, *that* question." She tapped a finger to her jaw, her eyes laughing. "How do I know you don't just want my backyard?"

"Pave the whole thing over. I don't care. All I want is you."

She took his face between her hands and bent to kiss him so thoroughly he nearly toppled. "Peter Santoro, I love you more than life itself. I'd be honored to be your wife."

He rose and slid the diamond on her finger. It fit beautifully, and he couldn't resist kissing her fingers. "I love you, Sadie."

"It's gorgeous," she whispered. "For this, I just might be able to give you a little piece of my backyard for a garden." She kissed him. "*Our* backyard."

ᴐ–ᶜᶜ

PETER'S HAND was only so much comfort against Sadie's lower back as they entered the community center the next afternoon. She blinked at the crowd. "Are you seriously related to all these people?"

He chuckled. "Seriously am. But you've met nearly everyone already, so there are just a few new faces for you. I'd like you to meet my cousin Rob and his family — they've come from Helena — and my uncle and aunt are here from Galena Landing. Oh, and that's my cousin Tony over by the kitchen doorway talking to Aunt Winnie. He'll be moving here soon to open an Italian restaurant." Peter nuzzled her hair. "He's all about unconventional ingredients, like zucchini noodles instead of pasta. Color Nonna not impressed, but he just laughs at her. Says alternatives make for a richer experience or some such thing."

"Wow, an Italian restaurant I can enjoy. That'll be great. Oh, look, there's your cousin Fran. I haven't seen her in a while." Sadie tugged Peter across the space. "Hi, Fran!"

Fran gave her an enthusiastic squeeze then held her away to look at her. "I heard a rumor about you."

Sadie couldn't wipe the grin off her face. "Don't believe everything you hear."

Fran grabbed Sadie's left hand and lifted it. She squealed. "It *is* true! You guys!" She let out a shrill whistle and held up Sadie's hand as though she were announcing a winner. "Congratulations are in order over here!"

Peter slid his arm around Sadie's waist as the clan swooped in with hugs and best wishes.

"When's the big day?" asked Aunt Genevera.

Sadie smiled up at Peter. "Probably next November. We've got a lot to do before then." Not that she wanted to wait an entire year, but they'd decided to be realistic. February was too soon and, once the growing season started, Peter would be too busy to take time off for a honeymoon until the harvest was in. Besides, she wanted to lose more of the weight that had clung to her since childhood. She'd made a good start, but there was still a long way to go. The counseling sessions would also continue a long while yet.

Nonna elbowed her way closer. "It is about time you

claim this woman, Pietro. Didn't I tell you she was the one for you?"

Sadie felt a flush creep up her cheeks as she glanced up at Peter, but he only laughed.

"You did, Nonna, and you were right. As usual."

"You will come to my house at Christmas Eve?"

Peter had told her Marietta usually hosted a drop-in gathering.

"Not this year. We're flying to Illinois to spend Christmas with Sadie's mom. Her dad is coming with us."

And she'd even be able to fit into an airplane seat. That was a miracle in itself, to say nothing of another restorative journey-in-progress. She and Jackie had spoken on the phone quite a few times since July, but she'd chosen not to visit in August.

Jasmine looped her arm through Sadie's. "Sorry, Nonna. I need to steal Sadie. She hasn't met some of the cousins yet, and Dad will be calling everyone to the tables any minute. Although I believe he's waiting on you to make the gravy."

"*Si*. The gravy." Marietta turned toward the kitchen at the back of the community center.

The place was bustling. Forty or fifty people surged around the room, hugging, laughing, and talking. Four generations of Santoros, with the littlest ones toddling after the bigger kids.

From on her own with an awkward relationship with her adoptive dad to a clan this size? Sadie had never seen it coming. Her heart swelled in gratitude for what God had done in her life since her move to Bridgeview.

Jasmine dragged her to one side and leaned in close.

"We've got an announcement today, too, but I don't want to steal your thunder."

Sadie whirled and grabbed both Jasmine's arms. "You're pregnant!"

"Peter's going to kill me." Jasmine giggled. "We're due in May, right when everything gets crazy busy in Bridgeview Backyards."

"Good thing we're not planning a summer wedding then."

"No kidding." Jasmine searched her face. "Are you okay with it?"

"Your baby or a fall wedding? I'm okay with both. More than okay. I'm so happy for you and Nathan."

Jasmine squeezed her. "And we're so happy for you."

Dancing at Daybreak

— An Urban Farm Fresh Romance 7 —

VALERIE COMER

GreenWords Media

CHAPTER 1

Dancing at Daybreak
An Urban Farm Fresh Romance 7

*M*ama, why don't you live here anymore?"

Dixie Wayling set down her fashion magazine and looked over at her five-year-old daughter. Mandy's messy blond hair curtained her face as she bent over a drawing at the table, empty cereal bowls pushed to the side. Dixie listened for the boys for a second but tuned them out when she heard two little voices from the backyard. No one was screaming. All was well.

Mandy pushed her tangles aside and looked at Dixie. "I miss you, Mama."

"Hey, baby, I'm right here."

"But you're not here to tuck me in at night time. Daddy doesn't sing me songs."

"His name is Dan. He's not your daddy." Dixie pulled to her feet. Why did her kid have to talk like this? Oh, she knew. She knew she'd taken the coward's way out... not only once, but a pile of times. She was a poor excuse for humanity. Mom had told her that since she was a kid, and it was true. About the only thing she did well was make more humans... a skill frowned upon by those who thought she should get settled, get married, and get religion, not necessarily in that order.

"God doesn't care about your past," Dan had said earnestly. "He's ready to forgive you and welcome you into His family. He did it for me, and He wants to do it for you. You just have to ask."

So, she'd kicked him out. She'd been getting tired of him, anyway. But then he found out she'd gone off drinking with her girlfriends and forgotten to get a sitter — wasn't Mandy old enough to watch her little brothers? — and returned the favor. He'd moved back in with the kids and told her she could either leave or marry him.

Such romance.

She'd stormed out, but the welcome at Mom's had worn thin after the first couple of weeks. Now she spent most daytimes with the boys while Mandy went to school and Dan to work. Sometimes he dropped them off at a neighborhood daycare instead, but he said her kids needed her more.

She watched them for no pay, like before, only now she had expenses. Of course, she *had* given birth to them. They weren't really Dan's responsibility in any way, except for the youngest. Who knew freewheeling party man Dan Ranta would turn into a grownup when she got pregnant with his kid? He sold used cars back then, and steady jobs were handy for paying rent and buying new clothes. But then his estranged father had a heart attack, and Dan found himself back in the fold, running the family landscaping business.

More money and an actual rental house instead of a dinky apartment had been kind of nice at first, until Dan *found Jesus*. Dixie bit back a snort.

Chewing on the end of a pencil crayon, Mandy watched her mama from deep brown eyes. "Daddy says he wants to have a wedding, and we can be a real family like everybody else."

Dixie crossed the space, kicking one of Henry's shoes into a pile of plastic blocks. She glanced out the patio door in time to see Buddy give the toddler a shove and send him to his diapered rear in the yellowing grass. No screaming. Whew. Dan had done a good thing getting them this house. The yard was kid-proof with not even a gate, so they could let the kids in and out without any worry. Dixie wasn't *that* bad a mother. She wouldn't let them loose in the wild without supervision.

She turned back to Mandy and tried to force her fingers through the tangles. "Run get a brush. You look a mess."

"Okay, Mama." Mandy slid off the chair and darted up the stairs.

Dixie picked up the drawing her daughter had been working on. It seemed to contain a humanoid shape, legs and arms outstretched, wearing a... tutu?

Something stabbed deep inside her, not for the first time. She was missing so much of her kids' younger years. Mandy had been in kindergarten for a month already, and Dixie hadn't even met her teacher. Dan dropped Mandy off at Bridgeview Elementary on his way to work and arranged for an older neighbor kid to walk her home every afternoon in case Henry was napping.

Dan was so considerate. He really was a nice guy. He might even pay for dance lessons for Mandy if Dixie asked. He'd been such a pushover, until he asked Dixie to marry him, and she said no. Because of the Jesus thing. Dan had only gotten guilty about them living together. She'd also said no because her mom's words rang in her ear, that she didn't need no man. It was Mom's favorite litany. Men were weak. Men were dumb. Men were needed for only one thing, and wasn't the planet full enough with over seven billion inhabitants? Then she'd look at Dixie's three kids and shake her head, her lips pursed in disapproval.

Yeah, pleasing Mom was impossible anyway. Pleasing Jesus would be no easier. Dixie might not be the sharpest crayon in the box, but she knew she wasn't good enough for God, no matter what Dan said about repentance and forgiveness and all that. He'd never been as bad as her. There were limits to what God could excuse.

I mean, look at me and my mess.

Mandy clattered down the stairs, neon pink hairbrush in hand. "Here, Mama. Don't pull too hard. It hurts my head." She slid back on the chair, her back to Dixie.

Dan had threatened to chop off Mandy's hair to make it easier to care for, but he was a pushover for the little girl's tears and had relented. Then he'd seen a YouTube video where some guy vacuumed his daughter's hair into a ponytail, and now he was all pro. But today was Saturday, and he'd left the house with the kids still in their pajamas.

Dixie didn't mind doing Mandy's hair once in a while.

She tugged the brush through the lower snarls and worked her way up to the scalp. Then she fingered the long strands into sections.

Mandy's hands covered hers. "What are you doing, Mama?"

"Thought I'd give you a French braid. Would you like that?"

"Oh! Can you? Autumn's mommy makes her hair into a crown for dance. It's so pretty."

Her daughter was five-and-a-half and Dixie hadn't braided her hair in so long Mandy couldn't remember? Failure two thousand three hundred eighty five as a mother. Not that she was keeping count.

$\backsim$

DAN RANTA PULLED his landscaping truck into the drive beside Dixie's older car. She was still here. Good. Ever since that time in July when the neighbor called him because Dixie had left the kids alone, he worried all day, every day. A guy could only do so much. He had a business to run. He needed the work to keep a roof over their heads and some stability for those young lives. He might not be Mandy or Buddy's biological father, but they were his responsibility now, and he wasn't the shirking kind.

If only...

Dan shook his head, shoved the truck door open, grabbed his backpack and lunchbox, and headed for the house. He eased the door open, braced against what he might find.

No one was yelling or crying. Mandy's giggle mingled

with Dixie's. He hadn't heard that in a long, long time. A breath slid out. *Thank You, Jesus.*

He tried not to take moments of harmony for granted. Tried not to segment each day in columns with bad, okay, and good as headers. He set his things inside the door and toed off his grass-stained steel-toed boots.

"Daddy's home!" Buddy charged down the short hallway and flung himself at Dan's knees.

Dan stiffened for impact as well as for Dixie's voice reminding the boy that he wasn't his daddy. For once, she skipped the opportunity. "Hey, Buddy!" He swung the almost-four-year-old into his arms and gave him a whisker rub. "Been good for your mama today?"

"Buddy always good."

Not to hear Dixie tell it... or from Dan's own experience. He chuckled. "Good job. What did you do?"

"Me'n Henry play tag."

Dan cringed. Didn't that just sound like a way for the bigger boy to chase and hit the smaller one? But, the toddler wasn't crying. At least, not right now. Dan dangled a squealing Buddy under his arm as he entered the living room beyond the staircase.

Dixie and Mandy looked up from the book they were reading on the sofa, and Mandy jumped up and ran over.

He hugged her against his leg, noting the braided crown, as he set Buddy down. Henry toddled over and Dan gave the little guy a quick hug as well. But his gaze was riveted on the children's mother.

Dixie looked happier today than sometimes, and he couldn't help smiling back. Her blond hair brushed the front of her top. He loved that one on her. Had he ever told her? But this might not be the moment, since the white lace reminded him of a wedding dress, and she'd shot that dream down in a big fat hurry every time he'd brought it up.

Dixie bit her lip as she took in the little ones crowding around him. Her eyebrows peaked as her gaze collided with his for an instant. "Hey, Dan." She surged off the couch and grabbed her big red purse. "I thought you'd never get here. See you Monday."

"Stay for dinner? I brought pizza. It's in the truck."

She smoothed the lacy top over her narrow hips with her free hand. "No, that's okay. I'm going out with some friends."

"Stay, Mama!" Mandy dashed back to her mother and clung to her arm. "Maybe we can watch a movie. Please?"

Dixie patted the little girl's back. "Not this time, baby. I have to go."

"I'll walk you out." Dan held the toddler to Mandy, who slung the little guy to her nonexistent hip.

"Not necessary."

"I know, but I have to grab the pizza, anyway."

Dixie skirted around him. "Suit yourself."

He hurried after her and opened the door as he shoved his feet into worn sneakers. "Dixie, wait."

But she didn't. He caught up to her beside the gray Mazda. "How's it running?"

She rolled her eyes. "Fine, Dan. It's not your responsibility."

"Sure, it is. I bought it for you."

"You want it back? Is that what this is all about?"

Dan let out a sharp breath. "No, of course not. It's yours, no matter what. I only care about you." He longed to sweep his fingers over her cheek, feel the petal-soft skin one more time. "Looks like you and the kids had a good day?"

"It was okay."

"Mandy's hair looks pretty."

Dixie shrugged, still not meeting his gaze. "Yeah. I remembered how. It made her happy."

"Thanks." Dan jammed his hands into his jeans pockets. In the old days when she got pouty like this, he'd have just kissed her until she smiled. Or maybe taken her off to bed. But he'd had a come-to-Jesus experience a couple of months ago, and he was determined to treat her with respect, whether she made it easy or not.

She wasn't making it easy.

Not sashaying in those skinny jeans and snug top. Not when she alternated between playing hard-to-get and throwing herself at him. Today was ice. He never knew ahead of time. The only things she was consistent about these days were jabbing at his newfound faith every chance she got... and refusing to marry him.

He took a breath. "I wanted to talk to you about Buddy's birthday. It's in just a couple of weeks. October second, right?"

"Yeah." She reached for the door handle.

Dan stayed in her way, and she pulled her hand back. "What do you want to do for a party?"

Dixie stared up at him. "He's just a little kid. He doesn't need a fuss."

"Fran Amato's little boy, Luca, turned four a few weeks ago, and she had a party for him."

He could see the battle on Dixie's face. Even she hadn't been able to come up with any evidence to support her earlier theory that Fran was his other girlfriend. Fran was a nice, married woman from Bridgeview Bible Church who ran a private daycare in her home a few blocks away. She was Dan's backup plan for the boys on days Dixie didn't show before he had to leave for work... which was once or twice a week.

"How nice for them."

That was all Dixie could come up with? He pushed ahead. "I don't really want to do a party with a bunch of little kids, but how about a family time on a Sunday afternoon? We could get pizza and go to a playground or the children's museum, maybe?"

He hated the need that came through in his voice. He hated putting himself at Dixie's mercy. He hated that he had to beg her to spend time with not just her kids, but him.

She stepped closer and rested her hands on his chest, sweat-stained T-shirt and all. "Maybe."

Dan stilled, forcing his hands to stay deep in his pockets as he inhaled the sweet fragrance of her. It took a minute before he could trust his voice. "What kind of maybe?"

"Quit with the Jesus talk, and we can go back to how things were before." Her fingers walked across his chest, each leaving a pinpoint of pain. "We were good together."

He took a big step backward and collided with the trash can, which clattered to the ground. The lid held. Good. "Don't use me as a pawn against the kids, Dix. They don't deserve it. They deserve a mom who's part of their life. Marry—"

"No." Dixie leaned into his face. "That's not how this game works, Daniel Ranta. You want to win? You've got the magic card in *your* hand. Play it." She pivoted on her heel, jerked the car door open, and climbed inside.

Without a backward glance, she drove away, taking Dan's heart with her.

Thanks for reading *Raindrops on Radishes*! I'm so honored that you chose to spend the last few hours with Sadie, Peter, and me. You are appreciated.

I'm an independent author who relies on my readers to help spread the word about stories you enjoy. Would you take a few minutes to let your friends know? Facebook, Twitter, Goodreads... wherever you hang out online.

Also, each honest review at online retailers means a lot to me and helps other readers know if this is a book they might enjoy. I'd sure appreciate your help getting word out.

I welcome contact from readers. At my website, you can contact me via email, read my blog, and find me on social media. You can also sign up for my newsletter to be notified of new releases, contests, special deals, and more! You'll receive *Promise of Peppermint*, the novella that introduces Bridgeview — Rebekah and Wade's story — absolutely free as my thank you gift!

Blessings, Valerie Comer

ABOUT VALERIE COMER

Valerie Comer's life on a small farm in western Canada provides the seed for stories of contemporary Christian romance. Like many of her characters, Valerie grows much of her own food and is active in the local foods movement as well as her church. She only hopes her imaginary friends enjoy their happily-ever-afters as much as she does hers, shared with her husband, adult kids, and adorable grand-daughters.

Valerie is a *USA Today* bestselling author and a two-time Word Award winner. She writes engaging characters, strong communities, and deep faith into her green clean romances.

To find out more, visit her website at www.valeriecomer.com, where you can read her blog, explore her many links, and sign up for her monthly email newsletter, where you will find news, giveaways, deals, book recommendations and more. You can also find Valerie blogging with other authors of Christian contemporary romance at Inspy Romance.